captain
– my –
captain

DEBORAH MEROFF

ZONDERVAN PUBLISHING HOUSE
GRAND RAPIDS • MICHIGAN

This book is published by the Zondervan Publishing House
1415 Lake Drive, S.E., Grand Rapids, Michigan 49506

CAPTAIN, MY CAPTAIN

Library of Congress Cataloging in Publication Data

Meroff, Deborah.
    Captain, my captain.

    Bibliography: p.
    1. Patten, Mary Anne Brown, 1837–1861—Fiction. 2. Patten, Joshua
A., 1826 or 7–1857—Fiction. 3. Neptune's Car (Clipper ship)—Fiction. I.
Title.
PS3563.E7424C36   1985   813'.54   85-22602
ISBN 0-310-41551-9

Edited by David Hazard
Designed by Kim Koning

Printed in the United States of America

85 86 87 88 89 90 / 10 9 8 7 6 5 4 3 2 1

FOR MY CAPTAIN

CONTENTS

part 1

THE LAUNCHING

"All is finished! And at length
Has come the bridal day
Of beauty and of strength.
Today the vessel shall be launched!"

—Henry Wadsworth Longfellow

chapter
1

The train lurched into motion. Sitting as I was, on the edge of my seat, the jolt catapulted me into the laps of two ladies sitting opposite me. They shrieked as though they were being murdered. I extracted myself with profuse apologies, and rubbed a patch of frost from the window. Alas, all I could see of my dear family was a huddle of cloaks and topcoats on the station platform. Then that glimpse, too, was blotted out by the swirling snow.

Andrew Brown, it's all your fault I'm on this train going to New York! I clenched my gloved hands and glared at the soot-blackened buildings lining the track to keep from crying. *If you hadn't rushed off to California with all those other gold-crazed miners you wouldn't have gotten into trouble. And you would never have met Joshua Patten.*

My oldest brother George had known better. He and Papa maintained from the first there was more money to be made at home. They warned Andrew he would be a fool to abandon his apprenticeship in the East Boston shipyards near our home. But my brother was seventeen and not moved by reasonable arguments. Nor was he touched by the tearful entreaties of my mother and my older sister.

I slumped back in my train seat, thinking of an early April evening four years before, in 1849. . . .

Andrew and I had walked together down Salutation Street and then along one of the wharves jutting into Boston Bay. The breeze was cool and the dark air smelled of salt and fish. In a few more days I was going to turn twelve and Andrew, the brother who had teased and bullied me all through childhood, would be gone. My world would never be the same.

"I don't want you to go, Drew," I said defiantly.

"I don't believe it. Is this my little sister talking?"

"You know I'll miss you. George never has time for me and Victoria—well, you know Victoria. We don't think much alike."

"That will change. You're growing up." He grinned suddenly. "Tell you what, I'll send you the first gold nugget I find. That'll put Victoria's nose out of joint."

"What if you don't find any?"

" 'Oh ye of little faith!' "

"Andrew, . . . let me go with you."

"What?"

"I promise I won't get in the way. I can help."

"Can you now? Just what every man needs, a little girl prospecting with him on the gold fields."

I burst into tears. "It isn't fair! Just because I'm a girl I don't get to go anywhere or do anything!"

" 'Mistress Mary, quite contrary,' " he mocked, using the nickname I detested. "Why don't you dry your eyes and look around you?"

Reluctantly, I turned my face upward, then caught my breath. Across the star-spattered heavens was flung a scarf of radiant colors, unlike any thing I had seen before.

"What is it?"

"*The aurora borealis*—Northern Lights."

"That's why you wanted to come out here tonight! You knew this was going to happen!"

He shrugged. "When nature puts on a fireworks display it's got to mean something special for whoever sees it. Especially if it's just before your twelfth birthday."

"Do you really think so? If only I could be sure!"

"You can be. You can make things happen, little sister. Don't just sit and hope life will come to you! Run out and meet it! And never look back."

A few days later, my brother was gone.

Andrew's letters home brought the gold rush very close to us all. Through his eyes we saw the hardships of the ocean voyage—the inadequate provisions, the greedy shipmasters. We learned about travelers who avoided the hazardous sail around Cape Horn by trekking overland from Panama to the Pacific coast. These men often met their end with treacherous native guides, swamps, fever, or starvation.

Those who did manage to survive the three-to-five-month journey encountered new problems.

"Eggs here sell for a dollar apiece!" Andrew wrote shortly after his arrival in San Francisco. "Boots cost a hundred dollars! I could not afford to stay here long even if I could find a place. Miners are jammed into every tent and shanty. Even the deserted ships are beached and used for hotels. I have thrown in my lot with two other prospectors," he finished. "Tomorrow we will set out for one of the southern camps and try our luck."

There was no more after that until just before Christmas. A package arrived, addressed to me. Breathlessly I tore it open and found a leather pouch; inside that was a small lump of gold.

Papa had the nugget made into a pendant for me. I wore it proudly until one day Victoria reproached me. "If you had any regard for Mama and Papa's feelings, you would put that gold piece away instead of flaunting it."

The accusation hurt. "You talk as though something's happened to Andrew!"

"We have to be realistic, Mary," my sister replied. "It's been over six months since we got his last letter."

"Letters can go astray. Or he might be somewhere where he can't post them."

"I don't know. . . . I have a terrible feeling about him, Mary. He should never have gone out there."

According to the newspaper accounts Papa had read to us, seven hundred and seventy-five vessels, carrying over forty thousand passengers, had cleared the eastern ports for California in 1849. Throughout that spring and summer the stampede continued, men lured from their jobs and families by the golden dream of instant wealth. And as George and Papa had predicted, the gold rush was also a boon for merchants and shipbuilders. Along the whole East Boston shore we could see new clippers, with huge cargo capacities and sharp, V-shaped hulls, rising in the stocks. Everyone wanted a share in the California trade, Papa said.

"It's an exciting day for America," he had mused at dinner one night, his eyes alight with enthusiasm. "There won't be a country in the world that can match our merchant fleet."

"Not a very loyal statement for an Englishman," George teased him.

Mama bristled. "Your father and I have been *Americans* since we set foot on this shore eighteen years ago! There's not a man in this country who has worked harder for it, with more love in his heart, than your papa."

And for the hundredth time, Mother and Father recounted

the story of their coming to America. As a young couple George and Elizabeth Brown had seen their lives being swallowed by the Lancashire mills, with no future for their small son and daughter. In a desperate move they had sold all of their possessions and bought a passage to America. Crammed in an evil-smelling hold with dozens of others, they had endured sickness and hunger. By the time the ship dropped anchor in Boston their first infant daughter was dead.

Survival in the "promised land" was not easy. Papa worked hard. When he was able to save a few dollars he bought some shares in one of the new ships being built. Eventually, the investments paid off, giving him the means to begin a modest ship's chandlery. When their second son was born, my parents proudly named him in honor of President Andrew Jackson.

"There is opportunity here for any man willing to work," declared Papa, pushing his chair back from the table. "Men are deceived by all this talk of gold. They believe they can pick their fortunes out of the streams without working for it."

Victoria dabbed her mouth primly with a napkin. "Robert agrees with you and Papa. He says the really smart men are staying here." Robert was the latest among her suitors, a dry-goods clerk. "In fact," she added, "Robert says he's sure to get a promotion because the senior clerk just walked out on his job!"

"Three cheers for Robert," I said dryly.

"*Mary!*" mother warned. It was her lot to mediate between Victoria and me.

"I just can't imagine why any man would choose to spend his life selling ribbons."

Victoria had grown pink with anger. "He's intelligent, that's why! Robert says there is no limit for the ambitious person in the retail trade."

"*Fiddlesticks*. If Robert was really smart he'd be out in California selling picks to prospectors."

"That's quite enough, Mary," mother rebuked. In the silence that followed, she added, "Sometimes I wish none of us had heard of California. Perhaps we'd all still be together."

There was more silence. Then I laid my hand over hers. "Don't worry, Mama. Andrew will come back to us soon."

And three weeks later—over a year and a half from the day he left—he did come back. With him was the stranger he declared had saved his life.

The train was shuddering to a halt. The sign above the station platform read *Worcester*, and I remembered that I had to change lines for Albany. I gathered up my carpetbag and hamper, and before long was settled on the next stage of my journey.

Unfortunately, over the clatter of the train, loud cries could now be heard from the hamper beside me. The two ladies I had fallen into earlier eyed me suspiciously. Suddenly I remembered the lunch my mother had packed for me and took it from my satchel. Raising the hamper lid cautiously, I pushed in half of a sandwich. The howling ceased.

"My cat," I explained to a monocled gentleman who sat across the aisle. He nodded and went back to his newspaper. And I to my thoughts.

In the days that followed Andrew's dramatic return that fall day in 1850, we learned that his gold-mining days had been very brief. Returning to San Francisco for supplies after his first strike, he had been set upon and shanghaied by a gang of land sharks, men hired by sea captains to round up crews. Like their other victims Andrew never knew what hit him until he woke up with a splitting head two hundred miles at sea in the forecastle of a sailing ship.

Fortunately for Drew, the ship's second officer had taken pity on his ignorance. He was shown how to handle himself alow and aloft, with "one hand for the ship and one for himself." But it wasn't easy. Life before the mast was the harshest kind of existence, calling for all his strength. By the time the *Albion* made port my brother was no longer a landlubber. He had gained a new respect for himself and for the sea; and he had won the friendship of the second mate, Joshua Patten.

The family, of course, couldn't do enough for the stranger. George and Papa invited him to their club. Mama plied him with her best cooking, and Victoria, who was being seriously courted by her dry-goods clerk, flirted with him shamelessly.

"I can't imagine what poor Robert thinks," I told her disgustedly after returning from a carriage ride one day. "You practically ignored him all afternoon. And then on the way back you insisted on sitting beside Mr. Patten."

"Robert may think whatever he likes," she replied vaguely. She was posed in front of the wardrobe, absorbed in the weighty contemplation of what to wear for dinner. "He will probably have me all to himself one day. I see no reason why I shouldn't enjoy myself while I can," she said, finally choosing a lovely blue satin.

"You are encouraging Mr. Patten unfairly."

"In case you haven't noticed, child, Joshua Patten needs no encouragement."

"Will you stop calling me *child.*"

"But you are! You're thirteen. Help me with my buttons, will you?"

"You're only sixteen."

"Did you see him smile when you started preaching about the Fugitive Slave Law? Really, Mary, I don't know what possesses you to to ramble on and on about such tedious subjects."

I flushed, yanking at the buttons. "It happens to be very important to a lot of people. But I suppose it was too much to expect a sailor to take part in intelligent conversation."

"Oh, Mr. Patten is extremely intelligent. He's read all sorts of books. Even poetry," she giggled.

I stepped back and eyed the dress. It looked extremely becoming on Victoria. But then, I thought gloomily, everything looked becoming on her. I found myself wishing for the thousandth time that I had the slenderness and fair skin that both she and George had inherited from my father. Alas, Andrew and I both resembled our petite, dark-haired and dark-eyed mother who, with her high color and quick temper, was often thought to be Irish rather than English-born.

"Well, I don't trust him. I don't think the rest of you should, either. What do we actually know about Mr. Joshua Patten?"

"According to Drew, he's from Maine. He went to sea as a cabin boy at age twelve, and he intends to become a clipper captain. He goes to church, doesn't drink, smoke, or swear. He's in his mid-twenties, average height, wonderful bronze skin and fair hair and moustache—but then you can see that as well as I," she smiled demurely.

"His eyes are funny."

"I didn't notice anything wrong with his eyes. They're blue, like mine," she said, seating herself in front of the vanity.

"Mr. Patten's eyes are *pale* blue. They're cold looking. You can never tell what he's thinking."

"I know what he's thinking when he looks at me."

"I don't like him," I insisted stubbornly.

"Better not let Andrew hear you say that. He thinks the sun rises and sets on Mr. Patten."

That was truer than I realized. After dinner that night,

Andrew announced to all of us that he had decided to sign on for another voyage.

"I guess I'm a glutton for punishment! Anyway, Joshua tells me the second time around is always easier."

Mother's fork fell from her hand and clattered on the plate. The news came as a shock. I had been so sure my brother was home to stay, that our lives would return to the way they had been before. It seemed that Drew was growing away from us. I felt helpless and hurt.

On the chill November day we gathered to watch him sail, I turned to my father. "Why, Papa?"

He shrugged. His eyes were on the vessel moving slowly out to sea. "Drew was always a restless lad. It's just something he has to do."

"But he could *do* anything, be anybody—a lawyer, a politician. Why must he throw himself away on the sea? It's Mr. Patten's fault, isn't it? He talked him into going."

"Don't be blaming Mr. Patten, Mary," said Mama. "It was your brother's decision."

George agreed. "Though Andrew could do worse than take him for an example. I liked Patten. Knows what he's after."

"I rather liked him, too," Victoria sighed. "I couldn't marry him, though. Sailors make terrible family men."

"Did he ask you?" I asked nastily.

"There now, lass," my father intervened. "Time to go home. Bad luck to watch a ship out of sight."

We turned our steps homeward over the cobbled streets. I wondered when we would next see Drew. Six months? A year?

"He *will* be back. I know he will."

And so, I had the sinking feeling, would Mr. Joshua Patten.

As the gray, winter countryside passed outside my train window, I wondered again and again how I had gotten myself into such a predicament. Why was I going off to meet a man who was still a stranger, and yet with whom my life and future were so bound? I was off on an adventure. I had no way of knowing, then, how much of an adventure it was to be.

The white hills and snow-covered trees of New England kept rushing by. As I moved toward my unknown destiny, I found myself drawn again to thoughts of the recent past.

chapter
2

The year 1851 saw important events taking place in our country, and Boston was the hub of activity. Two of the largest, sharpest clippers ever built were launched from Donald McKay's yard. The *Stag Hound* cleared a profit of $80,000 on her maiden voyage; and the *Flying Cloud,* living up to her name with acres of canvas billowing from her masts, sped from New York to the Golden Gate in a record-breaking eighty-nine days.

New laws were being passed. Prohibition went into effect in Maine and Illinois; women marched in the streets for the right to vote; and in the fall a minister's wife named Harriet Beecher Stowe published a novel serially in the *National Era* magazine that set afire the powder keg called abolition.

It was all tremendously exciting. I devoured every episode of *Uncle Tom's Cabin* and begged Papa to subscribe to William Lloyd Garrison's anti-slavery tabloid, *The Liberator.* The women's rights leaders were my heroines. So were courageous reformers like Dorothea Dix and the lone woman doctor, Elizabeth Blackwell. I resolved to be like them.

At Christmas that year Papa presented Mama with one of the new mechanical sewing machines invented by a man named Singer. Victoria was proposed to for the third time by the ambitious dry-goods clerk and she consented. I had asked for a pair of bloomers, but received a diary instead. I consoled myself by deciding to become a famous writer for the cause of liberty.

But 1852 was the year of new beginnings for me.

In February, Andrew swooped down on us like a breath of fresh, salt air. He looked hardier and handsomer than ever and no one could doubt that the seafaring life was agreeing with him. I even found it hard to resent his companion. Andrew informed us that Mr. Patten was now a first mate, and with all the new clippers being commissioned it was only a matter of time before he had a captain's berth. Looking at his long navy coat and brass buttons, I was impressed.

Mr. Patten appeared to notice a few favorable changes in me, too.

"You've grown up," he smiled. His grey-blue eyes took in my hair, swept back into a cascade of dark curls, and my fashionably tailored skirt and jacket.

I tossed my head. "I'm fifteen."

"Not for two more months, Mary, dear." Victoria materialized from somewhere, looking, as usual, like a Dresden figurine. "Poor little Mary, always trying to rush things."

"But you haven't told Mr. Patten your news, Victoria dear," I replied with saccharine sweetness. "My sister is getting married in June, Mr. Patten."

"Indeed?" His eyes moved from one to the other of us with amusement. "Then congratulations are in order, Miss Victoria."

"Thank you. Robert and I are just planning a sleighing party for tomorrow. You must consent to join us."

"Will Miss Mary be included in the party?"

She hesitated. "If she likes."

He bowed. "Excellent. I will look forward to it."

It was the first of many pleasant outings during that snowy February and March. Our sleighing often took us down Beacon Street and over the Mill Dam to Brighton Road, where we joined other friends for skating parties. Andrew escorted a different girl on every occasion—sometimes two girls at once—and was always the center of attention. I, too, had an assortment of partners. Most often, however, I found myself in the company of Joshua Patten. Did I enjoy being with him because I knew it irked Victoria? Or was it just fascination for a man ten years older than myself?

One evening Joshua took the family to hear Jenny Lind sing in the enormous Fitchburg Railroad Station hall. I was transfixed. The Swedish Nightingale was even more wonderful than the newspapers proclaimed. It was small wonder that at least two shipowners were planning to name new clippers in her honor.

The time came for Mr. Patten to sail again. Andrew yielded reluctantly to Victoria's pleas and agreed to stay behind to take part in her wedding. I accompanied my brother and his friend to the dock for the latter's farewell.

Andrew, to my surprise, murmured something about taking a closer look at the ship and ambled off.

"Do you know, Mr. Patten, it was this very day in April three years ago that Drew and I watched the Northern Lights from these wharves? Drew was about to leave for California and I was desolate because he would miss my birthday! And now you will miss it."

"Yes, I regret that very much. But perhaps you will accept a small present from me in advance?" He drew a parcel from

under his arm. "You've read it, I know, but you may enjoy
your own copy."

It was a first edition of *Uncle Tom's Cabin.*

"However did you get it?" I breathed. "They said every
copy was sold out immediately."

"Your father told me how disappointed you were. I
happened to have met Reverend and Mrs. Stowe in Bruns-
wick once. She was kind enough to reserve me a copy. It's
autographed, as you can see."

"You *know* Harriet Beecher Stowe?" I was aware that my
mouth was hanging open, and I must have looked every bit a
schoolgirl.

"Only slightly," he laughed.

I hugged the book to me. "I will treasure it always, Mr.
Patten! Thank you."

"It would please me if you would call me Joshua."

"Very well," I stammered. There was an awkward pause.
"You will come to visit when you're in port again? Mama and
Papa have taken to you, you know. Even George."

"And you, Mistress Mary? Do you want to see me again?"

His seriousness startled me. "Of course," I said, feeling
myself color.

"Good. Because I know I want to see you again, very
much."

He cupped my face with his hands and then, slowly,
deliberately, kissed me. Turning, he walked away, up the
gangplank.

I was astonished and thrilled. No one had ever kissed me
like that before. I touched my lips wonderingly, and turned to
find Andrew grinning at me.

"Happy birthday, little sister."

Victoria's marriage took place on a glorious day in June. When she and Robert moved to their own little house a few miles away, our house seemed quiet. And quieter still when Andrew joined the crew of a California clipper. It saddened me that our little family was breaking up.

During my visits to Victoria, she encouraged me to take an interest in some of the young men of our acquaintance. She was less coquettish, more content with life now that she was married, and she seemed to enjoy this new, matronly role of matchmaker. I wondered if I could find in 'marriage an answer to my own restlessness. Then I banished the idea. I was going to accomplish something Significant in my life. Resolutely, continually inspired by my rereading *Uncle Tom's Cabin*, I began to fill my diary with daring plans for reforming the world.

Joshua wrote one or two letters, friendly but impersonal. It would have pleased me more if he had written less of the details of shipboard life and more about himself. I felt there was a lot about Joshua Patten that no one really knew.

The winter of '53 was exceptionally severe. Late in January, we were surprised to receive a cable. Joshua was in New York, between sailings. He wanted permission from my father to see me.

I suppose that what followed was inevitable. Joshua Patten re-entered my life at the point when I was most longing for excitement and change. He had seen the world, and could talk casually about places the rest of us had only learned about in school books. Joshua set out to fascinate me, and he did.

With the approval of Mama and Papa, he took me everywhere—the most fashionable restaurants, museums, the theatre—sometimes with other couples and sometimes alone.

I found him an excellent conversationalist. He had a store of amusing anecdotes to relate, and he was conversant on most of the political and social issues of the day. I was gratifyingly aware of the envy of my friends for having such a sophisticated and self-assured escort. He made me feel older. Desirable. His nearness filled me with a strange inner trembling.

One evening in March as we rode home from a gathering at my sister's home, he was unusually silent. When I asked what was wrong, he told me that the repairs on his ship were being completed sooner than expected. He was scheduled to sail again the middle of April.

"But you can't!" I burst out. "That's less than a month away."

"I know, but I have to go. It's my job."

He traced the curve of my cheek with one finger. "Do you know what I am most afraid of? That I will leave and come back to find you gone. Betrothed to someone else."

"Never! I would never let that happen, Joshua. I love you."

"Do you?"

"Of course I do!"

"Then prove it. Say you will marry me now. Before I go."

"*Now?*" I drew back in shock. "Papa would never allow it."

"I have already discussed it with him. We can be married the first day of April."

"But I—I won't even be sixteen until the sixth."

He shrugged. "What difference does a few days make?"

I shook my head in confusion. It was all happening too fast.

"Does the difference in our ages bother you?"

"No. But Joshua," I faltered uncertainly. "Marriage is such a big step. Perhaps we ought to wait a little longer. After all—"

"*No.*"

His intensity shook me. "Trust me, Mary," he added more gently. "It's better this way. You'll see."

He drew me close, silencing my doubts, dissolving my fears. I made no more objection.

We were married two weeks later. The wedding was a simple affair. I chose to wear my mother's gown, trimmed with additional yards of satin ribbon and Brussels lace. Joshua sent me a circlet of orange blossoms to crown the long veil.

"You are so very young, Mary," Mama said, surveying the total effect after helping me dress. I saw the misgiving in her eyes.

"I wonder if we were right, your Papa and I, to give our consent."

"But you were no older than I when you married Papa."

"It was different with us. We knew each other since we were children. We grew up together. You and Joshua—"

"—have the rest of our lives to get to know one another. Don't fret, Mama." I gave her a reassuring hug. "I'm very happy. Everything is perfect, except that Drew isn't here."

During the short ride to Old North Church my confidence remained firm. Only when I heard the organ sound the first few notes of the bridal march did my courage vanish entirely. Suddenly weak-kneed, I clung to my father's arm in a state of panic.

Joshua waited at the end of the aisle with Reverend Smithett. He looked handsome and stern, but as my eyes met his the wild beating of my heart steadied. I listened calmly as the ceremony began. Then it was my turn.

"I, Mary, take thee, Joshua, to be my wedded husband . . . for better, for worse, for richer, for poorer, in sickness and in health . . . To love and to cherish till death us do part. . . ."

Joshua repeated the vows. Then he slipped the gold band onto my finger and I lifted my face for his kiss. Now there was no turning back.

For the first twenty-one months of our marriage Joshua and I were together for perhaps a third of that time. After the wedding we took a quick trip to Maine so that I could meet Joshua's family. Then he undertook several short voyages. It was not an ideal situation. Papa told me I was lucky not to be a whaler's wife, who could look forward to seeing her husband only once every three or four years. But that was little comfort. After each departure I was depressed and sorry for myself, lying awake at night and aching for the reality of his presence.

I took great pride in my letters, filling them with quotes from books I'd gotten at the new Boston Library, which opened in 1854. His own letters, alas, fell dismally short of the type a bride might expect from a lonely spouse. They usually read like jottings from a ship's log. *Heavy breezes and rain squalls. Made 310 miles.* Hardly the stuff of romance.

Victoria disapproved of my carefree existence. She lectured me continually when I went to visit.

"The trouble with you is that you have too much time on your hands. It's unseemly, always gadding about. One wouldn't think you were married!"

"I don't feel married." I twisted the gold band on my finger. "If it weren't for this ring I'd think I dreamed those weeks with Joshua."

"He had no business going off and leaving you like he did."

"Sailing is his profession, Victoria."

"Well, he should have at least seen you settled first in your own house. With a baby or two." She gazed adoringly at the infant in her lap. Her first child, Robert Junior, was making a noisy exploration of the room on his hands and knees.

"I am perfectly comfortable with Mama and Papa. As for children—motherhood may be well and good for you, dear sister, but it is hardly the only worthy function of our sex."

Victoria looked shocked. "You've been reading more of that women's rights nonsense, haven't you? What would your husband think if he knew?"

"Oh, Joshua knows. I copied all of Susan B. Anthony's latest speech in my last letter. In fact, I'm contemplating joining the American Women's Suffrage Association and Women's Anti-Slavery Society. The time has come for me to make my contribution."

Unfortunately, in January of 1855, my ambitions were cruelly severed. Joshua cabled from New York to announce that he had been appointed captain of the clipper *Neptune's Car*. He was to sail for California at once; and I was to join him.

It was all so unfair. Mama, Papa, Victoria, even George had acted as though it was the best possible news. No one had any sympathy for the fact that I had been asked—no, *ordered!*—to abandon everything that was most dear to me. Papa had practically forced me onto the train.

And now the train was coming to the end of the line. The conductor came through to report our arrival in New York City. Sighing, I gathered up my carpetbag and hamper and prepared to alight.

part 2

THE FIRST VOYAGE

"If I leave all for thee,
wilt thou exchange
    And be all to me?"

—Elizabeth Barret Browning

chapter
3

Joshua caught me by the shoulders as I stepped from the train and crushed me against his chest. "Welcome to New York!"

"I can't breathe!"

"I have no intention of letting you breathe for a full week at least." He held me away, however, to study my face. "I didn't think you'd come. If you hadn't, I would have gone to Boston and hauled you here."

"How absurd." I gave what I hoped was a convincing laugh. "Why wouldn't I? Everyone thinks it's the most romantic thing in the world that I'm sailing off on a clipper ship."

"And you?" His pale eyes commanded mine relentlessly, a smile playing on his lips. "How do you like the idea?"

"Well . . . I . . . it's all so sudden. I've hardly—"

"I didn't think you'd like it," he said, sounding not in the least perturbed. "But you'll have to get used to it. The time has come for us to live together as husband and wife."

"Of course. I agree absolutely. I've been so miserable without you, Joshua."

"Is that a fact? You've done a good job of concealing your misery."

"I wrote to you every day, didn't I? Victoria thought my letters were very moving. Especially the poetry—'The widest land, doom takes to part us, leaves thy heart in mine—'"

"'—with pulses that beat double,'" he finished. "The next time you copy Elizabeth Barrett Browning you should consider giving her some credit."

"How did I know you would recognize her?"

"That's not the point. The point is that a paper marriage can hardly substitute for the real thing!"

I squirmed. People around us were beginning to take an interest in the conversation.

"Couldn't we postpone this discussion, Joshua? I'm cold."

He frowned. "Very well. I'll show you to the carriage."

His eyes dropped to the wicker hamper I had set on the platform.

"What, may I ask, is in that basket?"

"My cat. You don't expect me to leave my darling Dix behind?"

"I not only expect it, I require it. I will not have that beast terrorizing the crew."

"Don't be ridiculous, Joshua. Dix only weighs fifteen pounds. You only have a grudge because she scratched you."

"There will be no discussion. The cat doesn't sail."

"Then neither do I!"

He let out a long-suffering sigh. "Be reasonable, Mary. The animal would probably hate living on a ship."

"How do you know? She might enjoy it. And you'd never have to worry about rats."

He continued to glower, but I knew I had scored a point.

"All right, but I'm warning you now. If that cat gets in the way just *once* she'll disappear over the side."

I clutched the hamper and murmured reassuringly as Joshua went off to claim my bags.

When he returned it was clear that his temper had not improved.

"Weren't you able to find my things?"

"It would have been difficult not to. They occupied three-quarters of the baggage car."

"You can't imagine how difficult it was to decide what to bring! In the end I just packed everything."

"Mary—"

"It is really your fault, Joshua, for giving me so little notice."

A silence descended. I looked out the window at the large number of fashionable carriages jostling each other, every one seemingly in a hurry to be somewhere else.

"New York must be full of wonderful places to visit! I do wish there were time to explore them before we leave."

"Sorry, my love, but the *Neptune's Car* has orders to sail with the morning tide."

Mention of his ship revived Joshua's spirits. He launched into a glowing description of the clipper while I listened politely.

"It sounds very nice, Joshua."

" '*She*.' A ship is always referred to as 'she,' " he reminded me. There was a gleam in his eyes. "Probably because of her tendency to stray off course without a firm hand on the helm."

"Really," I responded acidly. "I think it is more probably a tribute to her grace and beauty."

The carriage turned onto the street bordering the waterfront. I sat up straighter. Never had I seen so many ships crowded together in one place. Trading brigs, steamers, schooners, and clippers created a jungle of masts and riggings.

"There must be hundreds of vessels here," I marveled.

Joshua nodded. "It's a flourishing port—now more than ever, with the new railroad link to Chicago. New York transports goods to all the cities westward. If he's lucky a ship's master can dispose of his cargo to a single merchant and load again within days. In Boston that isn't possible."

Our carriage passed under a row of jibbooms that extended far out over the street. After another minute or so Joshua told the driver to stop.

"Look over there, Mary, beyond that pier. The clipper with the green and gold house flag."

I followed his direction. The *Neptune's Car* was riding at anchor, her sleek, black hull and tall, elegant masts setting her apart from the rest of the ships as distinctly as a thoroughbred among work horses.

"She's lovely!" And glancing at Joshua's face I was startled by its look of fierce pride and possessiveness.

"Are we to go on board now?"

"Yes." He took my arm. "There's a boat standing by."

The row took only a few moments but in the penetrating cold it seemed like an eternity.

"She is *big,* isn't she?" I said as we bobbed closer to the enormous hull.

"Two hundred sixteen feet long, forty feet broad, and sixteen hundred and sixteen tons. About the same size as the *Flying Cloud.*"

I could see the figurehead clearly now, a lifesized carving of King Neptune with long, white hair and a tumbling beard. He brandished his forked trident as though he were quite willing and able to pitch it at us.

"Not a very friendly old soul," I commented, and then was distracted by the sight of a narrow stairway affixed diagonally across the hull from deck to waterline.

"Good heavens. I don't have to climb that thing, do I?"

"It's the only way up, unless you prefer a rope ladder."

"Don't be facetious!" I eyed the steps fearfully. "They're bouncing up and down!"

"That's only the normal motion of the ship. I assure you it's perfectly safe, Mary."

"Ha! You aren't wearing yards of petticoats. How am I supposed to get onto that thing?"

"I'll show you." He leaped gracefully from the gunwhale and turned back. "You see? It's easy. Give me your hand."

I did as he said, then shrieked as ice water covered my feet. The oarsman snickered.

"I *told* you I couldn't do it!"

"You're all right." Joshua proceeded on up the steps, leaving me no recourse but to stagger after him. At last I stood on the deck, panting and shivering. A seaman lumbered up.

"Welcome to the *Neptune's Car*," he said belligerently, eyeing Joshua with a nervous, furtive look.

"This is our first mate, Mr. Buckley."

"How do you do?" I smiled determinedly and offered my hand. The mate recoiled. Mumbling something incoherent, he vanished abruptly down the main hatch.

"Well! Of all the rude behavior!"

"Perhaps he's just shy."

"That man obviously made up his mind to dislike me before I came aboard! You'll have to do something, Joshua. Dismiss him."

"If I dismiss every man who takes exception to you, my dear, I won't have a crew."

"But he doesn't even know me!"

Joshua shrugged. "It's nothing personal. You're a woman. A woman's presence on board is considered bad luck."

"How ridiculous. I thought that kind of attitude went out a hundred years ago."

"Some superstitions die hard." Then he seized my arm. "Let me show you the rest of the ship."

I allowed myself to be escorted to the foredeck. For the next hour, as the smile on my face froze into immobility, Joshua pointed out every rope, spar and gasket from jibboom to binnacle. Finally he wound up his lecture and led the way down the companionway steps to our cabin and ushered me inside.

"*Tea!*" I made a lunge for the steaming pot on the table.

Joshua looked disapproving. "I thought your first burst of enthusiasm might have been for our quarters."

The brew was heavenly. I cradled a cup in my hands and looked around in surprise.

"It's very nice."

And it was. The rosewood panels, the rich, brocaded furniture were a pleasant combination of charm and practicality that I had not expected on a ship.

"This is the parlor, I take it. Imagine having such a pretty tapestry carpet on the floor."

"Deck," Joshua corrected. "And it's called the reception room."

I ran my fingers across a polished mahogany writing desk, noticing the shelves of books above it. Everything was immaculate. I wondered uneasily if Joshua would expect things to be kept that way.

"Where does that door lead?"

"Into the saloon. We'll take our meals there most generally, with Buckley."

"Just the three of us? How cozy."

"The mates' quarters are just off the saloon. Also the passengers' berths, though they're unoccupied. Live freight usually turns out to be more trouble than it's worth."

I sighed. The company of others would have provided some diversion.

"Do we have a room for sleeping in, or do we sling hammocks at night?"

"I thought you would never ask."

He swept me up into his arms and, before I could protest, kicked open a paneled door and dropped me unceremoniously onto a broad double bed in gimbals.

"All the comforts of home, Mrs. Patten."

I laughed up at him, feeling the motion of the ship beneath me.

"I wonder if I will ever think of this as home."

"Of course you will."

The hot tea was beginning to make me feel sleepy. I closed my eyes, and the next moment felt Joshua working at the fastenings at my throat.

Six months is a long time for a man and woman to be apart. It is harder of course on the man; a woman has more powers of endurance. Nevertheless I must admit to disappointment when we heard a loud pounding on the outer cabin door. Joshua sprang away from me with a muffled roar.

"What is it, mister? It better be important."

"There's a longboat approaching, Captain. Looks like the same gents that was here yesterday."

He groaned. "The owners. I forgot. They wanted to meet you."

"The *owners?*" I sat up, clutching the throat of my gown. "How could you, Joshua? Look at me!"

He eyed me moodily.

"You'll have to make excuses while I change," I insisted.

"Shall I tell them you've been ravished by your husband?"

"*Joshua* . . ."

He kissed me.

"Joshua, the owners. Remember?"

Happily, the occasion was rescued by an excellent dinner prepared by the cook, who had been warned of the visit in advance. Mssrs. Foster and Nickerson ate hugely and then sat back, lighting cigars. I thought it was fortunate that Joshua was not addicted to the revolting habit.

"Splendid meal, Patten, splendid. Crack ship, fine fare, and a beautiful woman by your side! Many a man could envy you, captain," said Nickerson, giving Joshua a ribald wink. "No wonder you insisted on taking the little wife along."

"Did you really, Joshua?"

"He certainly did. The old man made it a condition. Said he wouldn't sail unless you went with him!"

I stared at him incredulously. He had risked everything with that condition. Why?

Joshua smiled and shrugged. "Just looking after our mutual interest, gentlemen. A wife shouldn't stay in drydock too long."

They guffawed appreciatively, while I ground my teeth.

"I'd drink to that, Patten, if you could offer me anything decent. Don't suppose you have anything hidden away?"

"No, sir. Even if prohibition weren't in effect I wouldn't have liquor on my ship. I've seen too much misery caused by drunken masters and bully mates."

"Yes, yes," Nickerson coughed. "Commendable."

"Whether you run a wet ship or a dry one is no concern of mine," said Foster. "What I'm looking for is results. Dollar and cent results."

The two men puffed on their cigars, measuring Joshua. The air of geniality had vanished.

"Your predecessor—Forbes. He took the *Neptune's Car* to Frisco in a hundred and seventeen days. That's good time but not good enough. You have to be a driver, Patten. It's the first ship into port that wins the best cargo prices. And the charters."

"I understand that, sir."

"Rumor has it the *Elizabeth F. Willets* and Captain Follansbee's barque, the *Greenfield*, are sailing tomorrow."

Joshua's shoulders lifted. "The *Neptune's Car* will show them a clean pair of heels."

"Good. We're depending on you, Patten. If you can shave two weeks off Forbes' time there'll be a bonus waiting for you in San Francisco."

The conversation and cigar-smoking continued interminably. At last the gentlemen rose to leave. Joshua and I stood on deck in the darkness as their small craft pulled away. I shivered.

"Cold?" His arm circled my shoulders.

"A little." How could I explain the apprehension that filled me at the thought of the long voyage ahead? I was in Joshua's world now, a different world than I had ever known, or wanted to know.

As though he read my thoughts, his grip on my shoulders tightened. "Come on. Let's go below."

"All right." I sighed. "Dix must be wondering what's become of me. And there's all the unpacking to do."

"The cat can wait. And so can the bags. I think we have some unfinished business."

I looked up at him and smiled. For the first time that day, I didn't offer a single objection.

chapter
4

I woke the next morning not knowing where I was. Then I heard the creak of rigging and the slap of water against the hull that was to become a familiar part of my daily existence. Were we already at sea? In dismay I sat up. Joshua's side of the bed was unoccupied except for a large yellow lump of fur.

"Dix?"

Her tail twitched but she refused to look up, and I knew she was registering a protest over yesterday's mistreatment. I reached over tentatively and stroked her head. She relented and began a strong, deep-throated rumble.

The cold of the cabin was numbing. With chattering teeth I hopped out of bed and rummaged in one of the trunks for my warmest serge gown. Should I wear it over my steel crinoline? Victoria would tell me that one should never lower one's standards of fashion, even aboard a ship. I fastened it on.

As I finished dressing the steward knocked. He staggered in with a tray heaped with food and coffee.

"*Buenas dias*, señora!" he said cheerfully. "The captain, he eats a long time ago. Now he waits on deck for the crew."

"Then we haven't left port yet?"

"No, no, señora," The steward laughed, white teeth flashing in a nut-brown face. He bustled importantly around, setting a place, pouring my coffee. I had never had anyone wait on me before, but decided I could adjust very easily.

"I am afraid I don't remember your name."

"Manolo, señora. Manolo Alfredo Vittorio Juan Torres Hernandez! At your service."

"You are from Mexico?"

He looked horrified. "Oh, no señora! I am *chileno.* From Chile."

"Oh." I sipped my coffee and munched on a biscuit. The steward did not seem inclined to leave, and I was wondering if it was the proper thing to dismiss him when Dix hit the floor in the other room and marched out. Manolo's grin stretched even wider.

"*Un gato! Qué grande! Qué hermoso!*"

"You like cats?" My warmth for the steward increased.

"Sí, señora! What is his name?"

"It's a 'she.' Dix, short for Dorothea Dix, a very great lady."

He bent down and patted her. Dix arched her back, receiving his attentions with dignity.

Shouts and a sudden violent rocking of the ship startled me. "What's happening?"

"The tugboat, she comes with the crew, señora. Now we go."

I looked regretfully at my unfinished breakfast. "I suppose the captain will want me on deck. Thank you, Manolo. Perhaps you could keep an eye on Dix for me?"

A few minutes later I was stepping from the companionway into a cold so harsh it sucked the breath from my lungs. Even the sun had a hard brilliance to it, touching the waves to sparkling whitecaps.

Joshua greeted me with a nod. I confess to expecting something warmer than that after our night together. Had he forgotten about it, or was he just being properly decorous in front of his officers?

"You're just in time to meet our crew. Fine-looking lot, aren't they?"

I stared, appalled, at the two dozen and more men that had just stumbled off the tugboat. A number of them were swaying on their feet, looking around belligerently. Several had already passed into the realms of unconsciousness.

"You don't mean *those* men are going to sail this ship?"

"They'll sail her. It may take a week or two to lick them into shape, but they'll do just fine."

The crew members slung their belongings over their shoulders and went forward to the deckhouse, prodded along by Mr. Buckley and the second mate. Suddenly one of the seamen balked and threw his bag down. The mate ordered him to pick it up. In a loud and colorful stream of language the sailor told him what he thought of the idea, spitting for emphasis. Mr. Buckley roared. Grabbing a thick wooden rod from along the rail he jumped on the man, thrashed him and laid him flat in a matter of seconds.

"Joshua," I croaked, "do something!"

"What do you propose? That man was half seas over. If Buckley let a challenge like that pass he'd have nothing but trouble for the whole voyage."

"But you're the captain. Surely—"

"It's the mate's business to discipline the crew. The captain is not expected to interfere."

I sighed and he glanced at me sharply.

"Perhaps you'd prefer to go below."

"No, I'm fine."

"As you wish. The shipping commissioner will muster the

crew for roll call now. After that I'll give them a little speech. That gives the second mate an extra few seconds to go through the dunnage for contraband."

"Contraband?"

"Whiskey. Firearms. Stilletos." Joshua took a few steps and then turned back. "Remember that you are never to go forward of this quarterdeck, Mary. That's from this moment on."

"Not ever? But what if I—"

"No 'buts,'" he cut me off. "For your own safety. And you are not to talk to anyone on this ship except myself, the steward and first officer, and, if necessary, the cook."

My eyes opened wide. He walked away to the rail above the maindeck and stood there with his back straight, his hand clasped behind him.

I seethed. Who did he think he was, talking to me as though I didn't have a mind or will of my own? It appeared that even the crew would have more freedom than I. For my "own safety," indeed!

The roll was called, then Joshua began briskly to address the men. His voice rang with an authority that brooked no disobedience.

As soon as he finished, the tugboat that put our crew and pilot aboard picked up the towing hawser and moved forward, ready to take up the slack. Back on the quarterdeck Joshua gave the order to heave ahead; the crew, at least those who were able to stand on their feet, began their laborious turn around the capstan.

One of the men broke into a chanty, and I listened, entranced.

Oh, the anchor is weigh'd, and the sails they are
   set,

> The maids that we're leaving we'll never forget!

The others joined in, timing their movement to the rhythm.

> We'll sing as we heave to the maidens we leave
> You know at this parting how sadly we grieve!

> Sing good-bye to Sally and good-bye to Sue,
> And you who are listening, good-bye to you.

On shore, clapping and shouting arose from the small crowd that had gathered.

> Come heave up the anchor, let's get it aweigh,
> It's got a firm grip, so heave steady, I say.

> Heave with a will, and heave long and strong,
> Sing a good chorus—

"Anchor's hove short, sir!" reported the mate.

Beside me, Joshua signaled the waiting tug to move slowly forward.

"Heave ahead, then, Mister Buckley!"

The crew threw their weight once more against the capstan bars for another round.

> The chain's up and down, now the bosun did
>   say,
> Have up to the hawse-pipe, the anchor's aweigh!

The anchor broke free of the water and was hoisted to the cathead.

"Anchor's aweigh, sir!"

Joshua nodded. "Ahead full speed!" The tugboat responded to our flag, pulling the *Neptune's Car* in its wake. I gripped the taffrail.

"The voyage doesn't officially begin until we drop our pilot at Sandy Hook," Joshua answered me. "There's a distance to go yet, through the Narrows and past Staten Island."

The crew were sent aloft to loose the foresails. I marveled that they could climb the ratlines at all, but Joshua's eyes narrowed critically, separating the green hands from the experienced.

"Look lively, lads! Make sail with a will!"

Topsails and topgallants were let go, canvas bellying out on all quarters. The mainsails came last, and as the men released the buntlines and the great expanse of white filled with wind, the vessel seemed to rise with a life of her own. The *Neptune's Car* was like a great bird, spreading her wings.

"The most beautiful sight in the world," Joshua murmured beside me.

The *Neptune's Car* raced for deep water, and we were soon through the channel and rounding Sandy Hook. The pilot boat was there, waiting. We backed our main yards and hove to discharge our pilot. Then, even as the schooner pulled away, our yards were braced again and we were off.

Off! Across the fathomless Atlantic, down the entire length of a continent and around Cape Horn. Then back up the other side—over fifteen thousand miles to San Francisco.

The *Neptune's Car* romped along, as joyously eager to put land behind her as I was to return to it. I stayed nailed to the rail, determined to remain there until the last beloved smear of solid earth was no longer visible. Joshua finally came up and shouted in my ear.

"Why in the name of sanity did you wear that absurd hoop skirt? Go below before you're blown inside out!"

"It's not a hoop, it's a crinoline."

"Whatever it is you will please furl it until the end of the voyage."

"I don't want to be down there by myself," I pleaded.

"What?" The captain's attention was distracted by an altercation between the second mate and one of the hands. "Just call the steward if you need anything, Mary."

I rolled my eyes. Clutching my bonnet with one hand, unruly skirts with the other, I leaned into the wind and took a few staggering steps toward the companionway. Then a hand closed over my elbow. I looked up into Joshua's face.

"Steady as she goes," he said, laughing at me.

Alone in the cabin, I hunched by the little coal stove and gave myself up to despair. How could I endure it? Four months confined to this wretched, tossing ship with no one to talk to but that arrogant lord of the quarterdeck and an ill-natured mate? It was like being shut in prison.

Dix came and brushed against my skirts, purring. Around her clung an odor of fish.

"Traitor. You've gone over to their side, haven't you? Got Manolo wrapped around your tail."

Some time later when Joshua came below he found belongings strewn everywhere and myself sitting listlessly in the midst.

"Mary, what have you been doing all this time? I thought you would have this cabin squared away by now."

"What difference does it make? There are weeks and months with nothing better to do." He strode over and in one motion set me on my feet.

"You will finish putting those things to rights at once, madam. I want our quarters shipshape by the time I return."

"And if they aren't?" I lifted my chin. "Will you send me home?"

He smiled grimly. "The only way you will leave this ship, my dear, is to jump overboard."

"It's an alternative worth considering!"

The door shut behind him. Sulkily I picked up some clothes and flung them into the wardrobe.

This was going to be a very long voyage.

chapteR
5

January 16, 1855

Dearest Mama and Papa, I begin this letter in the hope that
we will soon pass a homeward bound ship that we can give it
to. How I wish that I could deliver it to you in person! Your
daughter has been three days at sea, and I wonder if you miss
her as much as she misses you. A clipper ship is a lonely
place, especially for one who has grown up with the bustle
and excitement of Boston. It is a small kingdom unto itself,
peopled by men, with the captain the absolute monarch.
According to a manual I found he may "punish, put in irons,
or even take the life of any member of the passengers or
crew," should he deem it necessary! No wonder the men
stand in awe of him.

Mr. Buckley, the chief or first mate, is Joshua's general
overseer. His job is to keep the crew in line. He is also
supposed to keep a solicitous eye on my welfare—a duty he
regards with less than enthusiasm. Women, according to Mr.
Buckley (and, indeed, most of the crew), do not belong on a

sailing vessel! The man has taken a violent dislike to Dix, as well—probably because she too is a female. Thankfully, everyone else makes much of her and spoils her dreadfully.

The second mate is a young and cheerful Irishman named O'Keefe. I am not allowed to speak to him, which is a pity. His addition to the captain's table would be most agreeable. Alas, he is considered a sort of mongrel—neither an officer nor an ordinary sailor—and is obliged to make a second table from our own!

Shall I continue the inventory? Our ship carries a boat-swain, or bosun, who has charge of sails and rigging; a carpenter ("Chips"); a sailmaker ("Sails"); and of course a cook ("Doc"). Manolo is our steward; he is the captain's servant and is not called on for deck duty except in emergencies. This is fortunate for me for he is very amusing and we have become great friends. Joshua chides me for being too familiar with him!

If the captain is king of this little domain one might reasonably think I am queen. Unfortunately, this is not the case. I don't believe even Joshua has figured where I fit into the scheme of things. One thing is evident: I shall never be able to measure up to the standards of excellence he sets for everyone else. Captain Patten is a strict master and quite another man from the one we knew in Boston.

It is almost time to go in to dinner so I will close for now. Remember that you are all in my constant thoughts.

                              Your loving daughter,
                              Mary.

I blotted and folded the letter and, rising from the desk, steadied myself as a sudden lurch nearly overbalanced me. Was it my imagination or was the ship pitching even more than usual? At least, I thought, my appetite was unaffected by my trials. Eating was a great comfort.

As I entered the dining saloon a few minutes later I noticed that Joshua's place was empty. It was not the first time. My husband obviously held the opinion that the *Neptune's Car* would run into disaster without his continual presence on deck. I had scarcely seen him since we left New York.

"Is the captain not joining us?" I asked Mr. Buckley.

"No, ma'am. Sends his regrets. Looks like we got a nor'wester brewin'."

"How tiresome." Resigning myself to the mate's limited conversation, I took my place opposite him. Manolo was ladling up some kind of soup that smelled heavenly. Mr. Buckley stared at me with a gleam of speculation in his eyes.

"Gulf Stream's tricky. I seen some mighty bad storms in these waters. Blow the hair right out o' your head."

"Is that a fact?"

I tried the soup. It was delicious.

"Yes'm. . . . I seen many a seasoned sailor lose his dignity when we hit the Stream," Mr. Buckley chuckled.

I sighed pleasurably as Manolo brought on platters of pork, cabbage, and broccoli.

"You will see that I have no intention of becoming seasick, Mr. Buckley. If you have qualms about partaking of such a meal, then by all means refrain. I plan to enjoy myself."

I did, thoroughly. I had seconds of everything including the dessert, a rich golden custard topped with cream. The mate watched with unflattering astonishment and made the comment that he had never seen a lady "stow it away" like that.

After dinner I curled up with a romantic novel and box of chocolates that I had had the foresight to bring with me. For a while I remained oblivious to the worsening storm outside. Finally, however, the chocolates slid off the side table and startled Dix into flight. I gave up and went to bed.

Some time later I woke and sat up dizzily in the darkness. There was a rushing, roaring sound all around me, and the ship was being tossed like a cork.

"Joshua?"

I groped on the other side of the bed but naturally it was empty. Why couldn't Joshua be there when I needed him?

I huddled with my knees drawn up to my chin, shivering with cold and fear. In the darkness every sound was magnified. What if our ship couldn't survive the night? What if we were one of those that went to the bottom and no one ever heard of us again?

"Mary!" The cabin door suddenly banged open and I saw Joshua standing there with a lantern.

"Are you all right? It's a bad blow. We've lost a jib and topgallant and the night is far from over."

"I've been so afraid, Joshua! And you didn't come."

"I'm sorry." His voice was brisk, but gentle. He lit another lantern from his own and hung it above the bed. "I would have come sooner if it was possible."

"But you'll stay now, won't you? Please!"

"I can't. Try to understand, Mary. The ship is my responsibility."

"What about me? I'm your responsibility, too. I don't think I feel very well."

"You'll be all right. Just stay where you are and keep warm." He touched the back of his hand to my cheek, then picked up his lantern and went out.

I lay back. Overhead the lamp swung wildly, casting weird shadows on the walls. A faint, sickening smell of oil escaped from it. Back and forth . . . back and forth. I watched, mesmerized. A clock ticked loudly as the *Neptune's Car* rose and fell with monotonous regularity. A cold sweat broke out on my forehead.

Somehow I made it to the wash basin just in time. Wave after wave of nausea clutched me. I felt sicker than I had ever been in my life. Finally I fell back on the bed, limp and trembling, only to jerk up again a few seconds later.

It was near dawn before a haggard-looking Joshua appeared to report that the storm had abated slightly. I was beyond caring.

"Do something, Joshua. Help me. I'm dying."

"I'm afraid there's not much I can do."

"Oh, I knew it!"

"Mary, you have a simple case of *mal de mer*, that's all."

"*All?*—How can you be so unfeeling?"

"I'm not unfeeling. But it's been a long night." He dropped wearily into a chair.

"Help me up on deck, Joshua. It might help. Fresh air."

"Are you crazy? A full gale blowing and you want to stroll on deck?"

I burst into tears. "You don't care how I feel. You don't want me to get better!"

Joshua jerked himself from the chair, stamped to the saloon door.

"I'll send the steward in with some tea."

"I don't want tea. I don't want anything! Just go away."

I sobbed into my pillow. I wanted to go home. I wanted my mother and my father to care for me. If only I hadn't eaten all that food! The thought of it sent another spasm through me.

"*Señora? Señora*, it's me, Manolo! I come in, *sí?*"

He bounced in before I could reply. He was carrying a glass, grinning cheerfully. "I bring you something to make you better."

"What is it?" I eyed the glass suspiciously.

"Only water, señora. With a little cayenne pepper."

"You want me to drink water with pepper in it?"

"Only try it, señora," he pleaded. "Good for the stomach. Fix you up."

"Absolutely not! Take it away, Manolo."

Crestfallen, he trailed away.

Joshua looked in around noon and informed me that he had caught a few hours sleep in an unused stateroom so as not to disturb me. If I preferred he would do the same tonight.

"Do whatever you like," I said drearily. "I won't sleep anyway."

"You may be surprised. The winds are moderating. Things should calm down a bit." He grinned suddenly. "Poor Manolo was upset that you wouldn't try his remedy. You should have. From what I hear if you can keep it down ten minutes it actually has a chance of working."

"You're laughing! How can you stand there making a joke when your wife is in the last stages of—" I doubled up.

Joshua moved quickly to support my head, resisting my efforts to push him away.

"You can't keep this up, Mary. You're getting dehydrated. Manolo is gong to make some tea for you and this time you're going to drink it."

He departed and came back himself with the tea. I drank it, watching Dix give herself a thorough cleaning before settling beside me on the bed, purring in full throttle. When she slept, I did too.

I woke fourteen hours later, astonished. Aside from a feeling of weakness and hunger—soon remedied by a plateful of eggs, toast and coffee—it appeared that I might make a recovery after all.

Joshua bundled me up, blankets and all, and carried me to a chair in the protected lee of the quarterdeck. It was a lovely morning. I breathed deeply of it, wondering at the gentle breeze, calm sea, and benignly smiling sun. It was as if the storm had never been.

"We're in warmer latitudes now," Joshua said. He nodded with satisfaction at the yards. "Skysail weather."

The *Neptune's Car* was wearing her full complement of sails and I had to concede that it was an impressive sight. I opened my mouth, about to say something conciliatory toward the mending of our ragged relationship, when the mood was abruptly shattered.

"Mornin', Miz Patten." It was the surly mate, grinning at me.

"Cap'n says you been feelin' a might green around the gills. Sorry to hear that."

"I'm sure you are, Mr. Buckley. You will be relieved to learn that my chances for survival are good."

He strolled off, still grinning. I glared after him.

"Odious man."

"You do seem to bring out the worst in him."

I watched the mate move forward, stopping to talk with a dark, muscular man on the foredeck who was directing the replacement of some of the running gear.

"Mr. O'Keefe, now—he would never make himself so disagreeable."

Joshua's brows arched. But whatever he was going to say was lost by a sudden cry from the foreroyal yard.

"*Sail ho!*"

"Where away?"

"Broad on the port bow, sir."

Joshua grabbed his spyglass and trained it on the horizon. Eagerly I scanned the same direction, shielding my eyes against the sun. And then I saw it—white canvas, no larger than a moth fluttering against the sky.

"Who is she, Joshua?"

"Can't make out her flag. But she's clipper-built, and outward bound."

"Might be she's from Boston, sir." The mate had come aft again. "Weren't no other clipper scheduled to double Sandy Hook same day as us."

"But if she sailed from Boston, a day ahead of us, that would put us just about even, wouldn't it?" Joshua's eyes were bright with anticipation. "Mr. Buckley, it seems that we have ourselves a race!"

"Aye, aye, sir!"

"Let's show our visitor what we're made of. Call all hands and run out the studding booms. Then wet down the canvas. Lively, now!"

The crew responded. Men jumped onto the ratlines and surged out along the footropes.

"I thought all of our sails were already set."

Joshua nodded. "All the standard sails. Studding sails can be risky unless you have the right weather. But they add speed. And that's what we want."

The men, I saw, were rigging out oars to extend the length of the yardarms. Each extension was to bear an extra sail. It seemed like a lot of work for a knot or two more speed. While some of the crew worked on ropes, others were busy wetting down canvas—an even more back-breaking task. An unending relay of water buckets were passed up the masthead to be dashed onto the sails.

"Don't you think it's asking quite a lot? I mean, just for the sake of passing another clipper?"

The crew chose that moment to burst into a rowdy chanty called "Whiskey for My Johnny." Joshua laughed delightedly.

"Does it sound to you like I'm asking too much?"

Men! I thought. They were all impossible.

The *Neptune's Car,* swelled with canvas, sped on scarcely touching the tops of the waves. Mister Buckley measured our speed at fifteen, then sixteen knots. Two men were needed at the wheel to hold our course.

"I can't take any more!" I shrieked from my deck chair, clutching the blankets that threatened to carry me away. Joshua tore his gaze from the top hamper.

"Why don't you go below?"

"I can't! I can scarcely stand up! You'll have to carry me."

"Impossible. I can't leave the deck now."

I was speechless. Had he forgotten my recent ordeal, the weakness of my condition? Wasn't he the one responsible for carrying me here in the first place?

Spray flew everywhere, drenching me. I sputtered and struggled to my feet. Giving Joshua an outraged look, I sloshed to the companionway.

Manolo was all sympathy but even he could not restore my humor. He wisely took himself off to the pantry while I curled up on the settee to finish the novel and box of chocolates I had begun before my decline. Several hours elapsed. I had sunk into a comfortable state of forgetfulness when Joshua could be heard coming down the companionway steps.

"No use trying to overhaul her, she's steering too far easterly." He threw down his cap, surveying my posture with disapproval.

"I thought you would have had enough lounging around by now."

"Surely," I responded icily, "I am entitled to some convalescence?"

"It's my belief you'd be more content doing something useful."

"No doubt you have something in mind. Polishing brass? Mending the rigging?"

"This cabin could use attention."

I shrugged. "Tell Manolo. That's his job."

"You're mistaken, madam. He will help with the heavy work, such as scrubbing the deck. But this is our home and your responsibility."

I shut my book and rose with dignity. "It's time for lunch. Shall we discuss this afterward?"

"We'll discuss it now. On my ship everybody pulls their weight. Everybody. Or they don't eat."

"You can't really mean that," I said, faltering a little.

"Don't put me to the test, my love. Starting tomorrow morning you will pitch in with everyone else."

It was unthinkable, of course, to submit to such tyranny. I would rather die first.

For the rest of the day I invented variations of the same scene: Joshua bending over my frail form as I expired, pleading—too late—for my forgiveness.

The next morning I woke to the smell of bacon frying. My resolution crumpled. I found Joshua on deck and told him I had decided his suggestion had some merit.

"A woman can make a real contribution aboard this ship. There are a number of things that need correcting."

"Excellent, you can start with our living quarters. They look like a typhoon blew through them."

"I hadn't noticed."

"When you finish that, you'll want to do a wash. Ask Manolo to boil the water and string lines on deck for you."

"Lines?"

"The clothes will dry faster on deck. You may as well air the bedding while you're at it, too."

"Of course. May as well," I echoed faintly.

"You'll find a collection of articles that need mending in the dresser drawer. Holes in socks, missing buttons, that sort of thing. Shouldn't take too long. Any questions?"

Why would I have any questions? It was all perfectly clear: He wanted to work my fingers to the bone. I shook my head.

"Right." He gave me a dazzling smile. "Too bad you missed breakfast. It's always scheduled for 7:30, in the saloon. We can't expect Manolo to bring an extra tray every morning, can we?"

I know what Susan B. Anthony would have done. She would have walked to the rail and thrown herself into the sea to protest the servitude of all females. Frankly, that didn't appeal to me. I remembered there were still a few uneaten chocolates and went below.

chapter
6

Sunday, January 28, 1855

My dearest Victoria, today ends the first two dreadful weeks
at sea. Can it be only two? I feel that I have already been a
lifetime aboard this wretched craft, and that if I look in the
mirror I shall see a wrinkled old woman. (Surreptitiously I
wiped a tear from my eye as I dipped the pen in the inkwell.
Joshua, sitting at the chart table nearby, didn't look up.)

Alas, life on a clipper ship is not the romance it is depicted
to be. Sailors are little more than slaves, under the mates and
captain. And as for myself!—gentle sister, I dare not divulge
the shocking extent of the demands daily made upon my poor
strength! However, I strive to suffer my lot bravely, as a
woman must.

Except for the most necessary work, Sunday is fortunately
observed as a day of rest. Did you know that Joshua is quite
religious? I'm sure it's not unusual for a sea captain to read
his Bible with regularity and as though he genuinely takes
pleasure in it. Thank heavens he is not fanatical. I think he is

disappointed, though, that I do not share his enthusiasm for such things.

Today he conducted a service for the crew, which is one of the captain's regular duties. I must say it made a pretty picture with Joshua standing on the main hatch, the crew around him dressed in their best duck trousers and jerseys. It was amazing how completely he held the attention of the men. He read a psalm that was very appropriate: "They that go down to the sea in ships, that do business in great waters, these see the works of the Lord, and His wonders in the deep." Then those who knew English sang a hymn. All very entertaining when compared to our sedate morning services at Old North!

But there is much to get used to, dear Victoria. I am sure that neither Joshua or I expected that marriage would present so many difficulties. You and Robert made it look so easy. But of course it's a hundred times worse having to live on board a ship, with no other female to talk to.

I dabbed at my eyes once more. This time Joshua chanced to look up.

"What are you blubbering over?" he demanded with the insensitive tone he seemed to use with me more and more frequently.

"I'm writing to Victoria. She and I have become very close."

He snorted. "That's something new."

"Marriage has made us put aside our petty differences. We have discovered a common bond."

"I suppose you mean you both enjoy complaining about your husbands. Understand one thing clearly, Mary. I will not have the intimate details of our lives bandied around Boston by your feather-brained sister."

"Victoria is not feather-brained. You were once quite smitten with her, if I remember correctly."

"She is indiscreet. I can see the newspaper headlines now: 'Clipper Captain Brutalizes Wife.' "

"Well, I have to confide in someone, don't I? I can't talk to you."

"Have you ever tried?"

"You don't care how I feel! If you did you wouldn't make a drudge of me. Do you think all I care about is washing your shirts and mending your socks?"

"You haven't been overly abused," he said dryly, and picked up his compass. I watched him draw lines and figures on the chart and after a while got up to look over his shoulder.

"Is it very difficult, navigating?"

"Not very. Just exacting."

"I expect it would take me years to learn." I noticed, with curiosity, that the ocean chart looked like an ordinary map in reverse, the vast, blank spaces indicating land. The water areas were crowded with notes regarding currents, depths, and wind conditions and latitude and longitude markings.

"It wouldn't take you more than a few weeks, if you applied yourself."

"But that's wonderful! I'll do it!"

He laughed. "The word 'you' was only rhetorical. I would hardly expect you or any other female to be interested in navigation."

"Well, why on earth not?" I demanded indignantly. "Women are endowed with intelligence just like men. I, for one, think it would be quite entertaining to be able to plot our course on a map."

"Chart," he said.

"Chart, map, what difference does it make? The point is—"

"The point is you cannot use sloppy nautical terminology and expect to master a science as precise as navigation. You won't get away with adding an extra pinch of degrees here or there."

"I could learn, Joshua. I know I could."

He stared at me, incredulity softening into amusement on his face. "You're really serious, aren't you?"

"You're always saying I should do something useful. I could help you."

"It is sufficiently useful to me that you act as my wife."

"Josiah Creesy lets his wife navigate the *Flying Cloud*, so the newspapers say. Are you afraid that I can't learn or that you can't teach?"

He capitulated, chuckling. "Very well, Mistress Mary. We'll give you a try at it since you're so determined. But only on condition you'll give it up if you find the business more than you bargained for."

I agreed. Secretly, however, I was determined to succeed or die in the attempt. It would be a victory for Women's Equality. Even Susan B. Anthony would be proud.

Promptly at eight o'clock the next morning I presented myself on deck. Mr. Buckley, Joshua told me, would start by instructing me in the use of the sextant. The mate bore the look of one in acute gastric distress. It was clear that he thought the whole project a scandalous waste of time.

"Why does *he* have to instruct me?" I hissed. Joshua's brows rose innocently.

"Who did you have in mind? Mr. O'Keefe, perhaps?"

The mate shuffled up with a large, triangular-shaped instrument. He thrust it into my hands.

"That there's the sextant, ma'am."

"I am aware of that much," I snapped. From the corner of my eyes I saw Joshua move away, looking pleased with himself.

"What you have to do is look through that little telescope that's attached to it and point it at the sun."

I tried it. "I can't!" I gasped. "The sun's too dazzling!"

"You're always supposed to pull that dark glass down over the end first."

"Thank you for telling me."

"Now, hold the sextant with your left hand, and with the other one slide the alidad—"

"The *what?*"

"This gadget here. Move it till you see the horizon in the little mirror under the telescope. Then tighten the alidad screw so's the sun sits right on the horizon."

"Got it."

"If you look on the arc now, where the degrees are marked, you can read off the sun's elevation."

"That's all there is to it?"

"That's the easiest part. When I take the altitude, the cap'n is below checkin' the exact time by the chronometer. Then he looks in the nautical almanac to see how many degrees the sun is above the equator at that time. After he subtracts that from the sextant reading he has our latitude."

"I see." I didn't, but I wasn't about to admit that to the mate. "Isn't the ship's position determined by both latitude and longitude?"

"Yes'm. You want me to tell you how to find longitude?"

"Ah—tomorrow. We'll save that for the next lesson."

Mister Buckley looked relieved. Another thought occurred to me.

"What if the sun doesn't shine?"

"You can still get your position by shooting the stars. And if you ain't got either sun or stars you gotta depend on dead reckonin."

"Dead reckoning."

I pored over Mr. Bowditch's *American Navigator* all that day and the next, but everything remained a maze.

"Don't try to learn everything at once," Joshua encouraged. "Concentrate on the basics, then the rest will fall into place."

Mr. Buckley waited smugly for me to admit failure. Knowing that drove me even harder.

The *Neptune's Car*, meanwhile, was making excellent progress. Strong northeast tradewinds were giving us average speeds of thirteen and fourteen knots and more, driving us due south with only enough easting to round Cape St. Roque, the eastern jut of South America.

Joshua was particularly pleased that we hadn't been stalled in the "horse latitudes," the area of variable winds above the West Indies. He explained how it had received its name in the 1700's, when colonists carrying cargos of horses to the islands were caught in calms for so long their water supply gave out. The horses that died had to be jettisoned overboard.

"Unfortunately," he said, "this luck of ours can't last forever. We're due to lose the trades any time. Then you'll find out about the doldrums."

I found out all too soon. The fine breeze that had been filling our sails began to die away the very next day. By noon there was only a vagrant breath of wind to send us scudding another few yards. By evening the wind died completely and the *Neptune's Car* had coasted to a stop.

"Now what?" I asked Joshua, mopping my perspiring forehead.

"Now we just sit and wait."

"For the southeast trades? How long will that be?"

He shrugged. "A few hours, a few days. Maybe a week. Who can say?"

I decided steamers were far superior to sailing ships. It was illogical to just sit helplessly, at the mercy of the wind—*and* the heat.

The equatorial sun glowed down on us like a red-hot coal, blistering the exposed backs of the men. It even bubbled the pitch in the deck seams. I wore only the most necessary articles of clothing and still felt as though I were clad in armor.

Joshua rigged an awning on deck, where it was only slightly less stifling than the cabin. From there I was entertained by the sight of half-naked crew members jumping into the cool green Atlantic. While one man kept a lookout for sharks, the rest shouted and splashed like schoolboys, enjoying themselves hugely. It was almost more than I could endure.

I should not, however, have envied them their holiday. When the watch went back on duty it was business as usual; scraping rust, painting, tarring, and oiling. The decks continued to be holy-stoned white on hands and knees, inch by painful inch.

At supper I attempted a protest.

"Is it really necessary, Joshua, to push the men so hard in this heat?"

"Idle hands are the devil's playthings," the mate intoned. I ignored him.

"If you could just put off the hardest work—"

"The management of the crew is Mr. Buckley's responsibility, Mary," Joshua answered, preoccupied.

I sighed, picking at the broiled bonito caught by one of the sailors a few hours earlier. Unfortunately, my appetite was not up to its usual capacity. Fresh anything, after three weeks at sea, was a real treat. Mr. Buckley consumed his portion with gusto.

Joshua's fist suddenly struck the table, startling us all.

"I'd give a month's wages to know where that other clipper lies!"

"Do you figure she's run away from us, sir?"

"More likely becalmed, like us. Three, even four hundred miles to the west."

"I don't much care where she is," I said flatly. "I just want to start moving again."

"There has to be a wind somewhere. Wherever it is, we're going to find it."

He rose from the table resolutely. "Mr. Buckley, have all hands standing ready to brace for every cat's paw. No more off-duty swimming."

In fairness I had to admit that Joshua did not drive the crew any harder than he drove himself. The need for speed was like a fever inside him. Ceaselessly he prowled the deck, scanning the sea for any ripples that might betray a breeze. It almost seemed that he was conjuring them by sheer strength of will.

Near sunset I went to stand beside him at the weather rail. Together we watched the fiery disc on the horizon dip lower and lower until it was extinguished, splashing hot streaks of color into the sky. Crimson and fuschia glowed vividly for a long time before yielding to gentler pinks and magenta—and then, finally, darkness.

One by one the heavenly lights blinked on. Around us the waters swirled with an eerie phosphorescence.

It was a night that would stir even the hardest heart. I was not surprised when Joshua's arm slipped around my waist.

"Incredible, isn't it?" he murmured. Then he quoted, his voice soft and resonant: "When I consider thy heavens, the work of thy fingers, the moon and the stars, which thou hast ordained, what is man, that thou art mindful of him?"

We stood gazing for a long time into the warm darkness. Finally he spoke again and my heart skipped a beat.

"A night like this is too rare an opportunity to miss."

"Exactly what I was thinking." A delicious shiver traveled down my spine.

"Good. Do you want to go below or shall I?"

"Go below?"

"For the sextant." He sounded surprised. "So we can try some celestial navigation."

I went below. I did not, however, return with the sextant. I locked the door.

If stars were all that interested Joshua, stars were all he was going to get!

chapter
7

To everyone's immense relief a breeze sprang up the next morning and sent us once more on our way. As we crossed the equator, Manolo told me I was now a "daughter of Neptune." Officially, he said, the occasion should be celebrated by the whole crew. I carried the idea to Joshua, who received it with a marked lack of enthusiasm.

"We're not a passenger ship. We don't have to be bothered with that sort of thing. It's too hot, anyway."

"Oh, Joshua, don't be such a spoilsport! It would be such fun to have a party."

"In case it has escaped your notice, my dear, this is not a pleasure cruise. There will be no parties, and that's that."

I sulked. If everyone else celebrated crossing the line then so should we. At least, I thought suddenly, we could have some cakes. I would bake them and decorate them myself if I had to, enough for the whole crew.

When Joshua went into the chart room I hurried to the galley. It really was insufferably hot. By the time I reached my destination my clothes were drenched and clinging to me.

The temptation was strong to give up the whole project, but annoyance with Joshua stiffened my resolve.

I found the cook lethargically peeling onions. It was the first time that I had ventured into his territory, and when he saw me his eyes widened.

"Miz Patten!"

"Good afternoon, Mr.—"

"Call me Doc, ma'am. Jus' plain Doc." His lips parted to reveal a row of crooked and tobacco-stained teeth. "Don' know why, lessen it's 'cause cooks is handy with the cleaver."

He brandished his and I took a step backward.

"That's lovely. I'm pleased to meet you, Doc. Actually, I came here to ask a small favor. I'd like to have a cake for tonight. Several, in fact. Enough for all the men to celebrate crossing the line."

"Celebrate! Ma'am, you sure? This ain't no time for bakin' cakes. This be a time for keepin' our own selves from cookin'!"

"I am sure, Doc."

"This stove ain't even fired up!"

"You could fire it, couldn't you? I'd make the cakes myself. You won't have to do a thing. Just show me where the ingredients are and start the oven, then go and find a cooler spot for yourself."

He scratched his head. "'Spose I could do that. Supper's mostly ready." He began to shuffle about setting flour and sugar on the table while I blotted my streaming brow with a handkerchief.

"There, now," he said a few moments later. "Fire's goin'. You sure you gonna be all right, ma'am?"

"Fine. Thank you, Doc!"

Moving very slowly I creamed together eggs and shortening, sifted in the flour, salt and baking powder. Six large cakes ought to be enough, I thought. An hour for baking, and I would still have plenty of time to cool and frost them.

The air in the galley was becoming hard to breathe. I wondered dizzily if the three Hebrews had felt the same way in the fiery furnace. *Concentrate, Mary. Add the vanilla. Now stir.*

A thick fog was enveloping me. My head pounded. Blindly I turned the heavy batter into greased and floured pans and carried two of them to the oven.

A fearful blast struck me as I opened the door. Forcing myself to move with enormous effort, I slid the pans onto the rack, then went back for more. The last two cakes were just going in when I heard an angry exclamation from the galley door.

"In the name of sanity, Mary! Are you trying to kill yourself?"

I straightened up. Instantly, a wave of vertigo overwhelmed me. I grabbed for the edge of the table and then Joshua was there, lifting me into his arms.

Tears of frustration came to my eyes. I wept, "It was . . . going to be a surprise!"

Then everything spun away into darkness.

I have no idea how much time elapsed before I became aware that I was lying, half-clad, on my bed. When I opened my eyes I saw Joshua standing over me, watching closely. I wanted desperately to turn away from him but somehow my body would not respond. It felt peculiarly weighted and heavy. Finally I moved my head a fraction and pain stabbed through my temples. I gasped.

"Is it very bad?"

I nodded and he went into the next room. There were sounds—something being poured, the tinkle of a spoon in a glass. In a moment he returned.

"Drink this. It will help."

Ridiculous, I thought, dizzily, *to be so entirely helpless*. Joshua held the glass to my lips and a liquid, cool and soothing, streamed through me. It was an incredible sensation. One moment to be crushed down by unendurable pain, the next, floating and deliciously free. Somewhere far away Joshua was still frowning at me, but it no longer mattered. I felt myself being borne away from his displeasure.

I did not wake again for many hours. There was a strong reluctance to let go of my woven strands of fantasy, but even as I fought to hold them, a voice kept intruding, calling my name with cruel insistence. It was Joshua's voice. Memory returned in a rush and I sat upright.

"My cakes! What happened to them?"

Hands forced me back on the pillows. "They've fared better than you. Now lie still."

I obeyed.

"That was a foolish thing to do, Mary. You know that, don't you?"

"I wanted to surprise everyone."

"So you told me, before you passed out. In actual fact it was a childish and headstrong mutiny against my authority."

Tears pricked my eyes. "That's not true! And I don't see why you should be angry. I've been punished enough for it."

"Yes," he said wearily, "I suppose you have."

"Did you—did you have the cake?"

"Doc served it at supper last night. He thought he should, after you went to the trouble of making it. The crew was delighted. You may find a way yet into their superstitious hearts. Even Buckley had a kind word to say."

"And you?" Somehow it was important to know. "Did you like it, Joshua?"

He stood up abruptly. "I'm overdue on deck. Manolo's nearby. If you need him, call."

The steward did not wait for a summons but popped in as soon as Joshua left.

"*Como está*, señora? That Doc, he's crazy. Loco." He tapped his head. "I tell him he should know not to let you do this thing. He should be fed to the sharks."

"Captain Patten is angry with me, Manolo."

"It is true he does not look happy, señora. Last night, he eats no supper, and then I hear him walk up and down, up and down. When I come in this morning to bring the coffee the captain sits by you in this chair. Maybe he is angry, señora, but I do not think at you."

"Who else could there be?"

The steward shrugged. "Maybe—himself, señora?"

I laughed. Manolo could not be more mistaken if he believed Joshua blamed himself for anything. But I didn't want to think about it anymore. Thinking made my head ache.

The feeling of lassitude remained with me for the next several days. Joshua, for once, made no objection about my inactivity and it was finally my own boredom that drove me to resume my chores.

Meanwhile, brisk southeast tradewinds filled our sails and we pushed rapidly down the South American coast.

"According to my figuring we are now at latitude 33°30', longitude 53° 38'. What do you have?" I peered at the log where Joshua had just entered his own figures, and gave a whoop of delight.

"I did it! I can't believe it! Joshua, we have the same exact position!"

"Come over and look at this chart, Mary. Do you see where we are?"

"Yes," I pointed, "right here, off the coast of Argentina."

"And opposite the Rio de la Plata. That may mean trouble."

Before he could explain, there was a knock on the door. Joshua opened it to a tense-looking mate.

"Afraid it's bad news, sir. Dirty weather headin' into us from the southwest."

Joshua and I followed him on deck. Off in the distance we could clearly see the massive black cloud bank spreading in our direction.

"Looks like a *pampero*, all right. Mister Buckley?"

"Aye, sir."

"Shorten sail to lower tops'ls and forestays'l. Drop over the lightning lines. Let's button her down."

"Aye, aye, sir!"

The wind freshened even while he spoke, whipping the waves to excited peaks. Lightning darted out, like the forked tongue of a serpent, and was followed by an ominous staccato.

"Joshua? What's a *pampero?*"

"Starts as a cold wind off the Andes, then it sweeps over the Argentine plain—the pampas—until it hits the river. When it does, there's nowhere to run. Ships are thrown into each other and onto the rocks. And it blows for miles into the sea."

I shuddered, watching the off-duty crew rush from the deckhouse and up onto the yardarms to furl canvas.

"You'd better go below, Mary. Secure what you can."

He moved toward the main deck and I started toward the companionway. Then I stopped, mesmerized. The venomous clouds were moving closer, roiling above the ship. Chains rattled, orders were shouted, and men scurried to obey. It was like watching a play. The menace approached, and I was powerless to stop it.

Joshua glanced aft and saw me still standing there. He froze.

"*Mary!*"

I saw the shout, rather than heard it. He ran back, gripped me hard, and shook me out of my trance.

"Get below! *Move!*"

Trembling now, I flung myself down the companionway and made the cabin just as the full violence of the *pampero* slammed into us. It was like hitting a stone wall. I was thrown against the bulkhead as the *Neptune's Car* rolled over. Down, down she leaned until she was almost on her beam ends.

"Dear God," I sobbed, "please save us!"

The ship struggled like a wounded thing, trying to rise against the terrible weight of the waves smashing her hull. And then, painfully, she began to roll onto her keel.

The storm was not nearly over, but now at least the ship could fight back. Wind, rain and hail lashed her mercilessly. I crouched on the floor in terror. The storm at the Gulf Stream had been nothing compared to this. I thought of the men on deck, wondering if they could possibly survive. I thought of Joshua.

No! Nothing can happen to him. God wouldn't let it!

Nevertheless, I continued to sit with the debris of books and papers around me. My eyes were fixed on the cabin door. And when—after what seemed like hours—it finally opened, I threw myself at the oilskinned figure.

"Thank God! Oh, Joshua, I thought for certain we would go down!"

"Steady, girl." He held me away gently. "You're hurt."

For the first time I noticed my torn sleeve.

"It's nothing, just a scratch. I'm frightened more than anything. Joshua, when I thought of what might be happening out there—to you—"

He was still, as if waiting for something more. When I remained silent he smiled and said lightly, "Clipper masters are immortal, didn't you know?—If you're sure you're all right I'll go back up and tend my ailing ship."

Joshua did not join me again until almost dawn. As he crawled into bed beside me he reported that a man had broken an arm, we had lost the forestaysail, and the mizzen masthead was sprung. One of the chicken coops had also been carried away and a lifeboat stove in. But we had gotten off "lucky."

"*Caramba*, señora!" Manolo, bringing coffee to me in the saloon several hours later, appeared a little subdued. "These *pamperos*, they are not so good, eh? And now comes the Horn. She is even worse!"

"*Worse?*" My stomach tightened nervously.

"Oh, *sí*. The sailors call her 'the graveyard of ships!' "

It was not a statement to quiet one's fears. I became even more alarmed as I observed the activity taking place all around me. Crew members were employed in an extensive overhaul of the sails, bending tough new canvas in place of the old. Every inch of the running gear was inspected, tarred and greased, worn ropes were replaced and buntlines and leechlines doubled up. Loose gear was stowed or lashed tightly under the forecastle head. And lifelines were stretched all along the decks.

In the saloon, Manolo busily attached fiddles, or wooden frames onto the tabletop to keep our plates and cups from sliding about.

"What a pity there are no such contraptions to keep us from sliding about as well," I commented.

Manolo grinned. "The señora, always she jokes."

I felt less like joking with every passing day. To keep myself from panic I began spending time in the galley, thinking up all manner of delicacies for the men. There was little risk of heat exhaustion now—the air was actually frosty. Feverishly I turned out bread, rolls, johnnycake, pies and pudding. Mr. Buckley's cordiality increased with every offering.

The spectacle of mollymawks and Cape pigeons wheeling noisily around the ship became quite common. It was the sight of homeward-bound vessels, however, that brought tears to my eyes. When we exchanged mail with one such ship we learned that we were only a hundred miles astern of the clipper *Westward Ho,* from Boston.

Joshua immediately ordered more sail clapped on.

"The *Westward Ho!*" I exclaimed. "I saw her launched from Donald McKay's yard!"

"She's a fast ship. Captain Hussey's a driver."

"Do you think we can catch up to her?"

Joshua gave me an impatient look. "You should know by now the *Neptune's Car* isn't easily beaten. I have every confidence that when we sail through the Golden Gate the *Westward Ho* will be under our stern."

I clung to the braces. At sixteen knots one had the sensation almost of flying. When Joshua went aft to exchange a word with the helmsman, Mr. Buckley's eyes followed him admiringly. I was goaded into shouting, "Was that wise— ordering the main royal set? How long can it last in this wind?"

"Can't say, ma'am, but I'll tell you this. Cap'n Patten's a driver. Most men would be sendin' down the royal yards and stuns'l booms this close to the Horn. The Old Man, he's flyin' every rag we've got!"

It sounded to me more like reckless irresponsibility.

A report like cannon fire jerked our gaze upward. It was the main royal sail, of course, blown to ribbons.

I said with some asperity, "I guess we have our answer, Mr. Buckley!"

Joshua, however, was unperturbed. I was coming to learn that nothing perturbed Joshua unless it seriously impeded his speed. I suspected that if I fell overboard he would see no reason to slow up.

By nightfall the gap between the two clippers had closed. When the lookout raised a cry of "Lights! Port bow!" every man lined the rails for a glimpse of the red glow belonging to the *Westward Ho*. And when the next morning, we filled away and ran ahead of her, they split the air with a tremendous cheer.

It was a sweet moment for Joshua. For myself, I could think only of what lay ahead: the Cape of Storms. And our passage through the "roaring forties" was to fulfill my worst imaginings.

chapter
8

To those versed in nautical matters, "rounding the Horn" means traveling from latitude fifty degrees, South Atlantic, to fifty degrees, South Pacific. The forties, however, are the terrible prelude. When one enters those dark waters, the hot equatorial sunshine is forgotten. It is the region of eternal storms.

I piled on my warmest wools and continued to shiver. Most of the time I stayed below with Dix as my willing companion. The spectacle of menacing skies, wild seas, and men balancing on ice-coated footropes did not allure me. One night, however, the wind fell away, and we woke in long, oily swells. Joshua persuaded me to come on deck. There he pointed out the Falkland Islands.

It was a barren, desolate landfall—but it was land nevertheless. After seven weeks at sea the sight filled me with a sharp longing.

"Oh, I do wish we could go ashore. Just for a while."

He laughed. "You wouldn't care for that place, I assure you."

"Anything would be preferable to this ship. I am so tired of it."

"Cheer up, my love. We'll be halfway to California once we round Cape Stiff."

"*If* we round it!"

"Haven't I brought you safe this far?"

"Safe?" I nearly shouted. "You call it *safe?* Seasickness, sunstroke, storms that nearly sent us to the bottom? Temperatures to roast us one day, freeze us the next. Not to mention all the loneliness and boredom I've suffered. And having to put up with Mister Buckley."

"And me?"

"Yes, and you." My chin lifted defiantly under his steady regard.

"Go ahead. Tell me you haven't enjoyed my company either. It's what you're thinking."

"Is it?"

"Just remember it was your idea for me to come on this trip. If it were up to me—"

"I know. You would still be moored safely in Boston town. But what if I had never made you weigh anchor? Wouldn't you ever wonder, Mary, what lies outside that snug harbor?"

"Why must you put everything into nautical terms? I am not a ship, and I won't be handled like one."

"You're right. Ships are more reliable." Joshua's eyes were a stormy gray. "Learn their strengths and weaknesses, respect them, and they'll do their best for you, come foul or fair weather."

"It seems it all boils down to respect, then, doesn't it?"

"Yes. *Mutual* respect."

I turned away. "Since that is impossible, I'll thank you to book my passage home the minute we reach San Francisco."

"Not so fast."

I winced as his hand gripped my arm. "I'll thank *you* to remember you don't give the orders on this ship. I'll be the one to decide if you can go. And where."

I was purple with outrage. How *dare* he treat me as if he owned me? In front of Mr. O'Keefe, too! I yanked my arm away and walked below. From now on there would be no more communication than was necessary.

But it is hard to ignore someone who hardly seems aware of your existence. Joshua seldom left the deck. All of his energies were bent on the challenge of doubling the Horn in the quickest possible time.

I knew that vessels could spend weeks futilely beating their way against the strong westerly winds under the South American continent. Not a few captains, faced with exhausted crews, dwindling food and water supplies, or crippling storm damage, had given up and turned back. Somehow I could not imagine Joshua turning back from anything.

As I studied the chart I saw a critical choice ahead. Joshua could let the westerlies blow us past Staten Island, then brace our yards against the headwinds and tack west. Or he could make a run for it through the Strait of Le Maire between Staten Island and Cape San Diego on the mainland.

The strait was shorter. It therefore presented a highly attractive lure to clipper masters. It was also a navigational nightmare full of tide rips, powerful currents and crosscurrents. I waited for Joshua's decision with the now-familiar feeling of dread.

"We're up against the calendar. We have no idea of the *Westward Ho's* position. She may easily have slipped wide of us in the squalls and fogs and run on ahead. If there's a short cut we take it."

"Oh, bother the *Westward Ho!* Doesn't safety count for anything? Passing through that channel is like—like threading a needle! If you miss—"

"I won't miss, Mary."

I sighed my frustration.

"There's some risk, naturally. But that's what skippers are paid to take. I don't intend to let anything happen to this ship or its crew."

The *Neptune's Car* pressed on, now encountering the frightful Cape Horn greybeards. Andrew had once described these monster waves to me. They curled a thousand feet in length and rose to heights of fifty feet—even the thought of them terrified me. I held my breath as, time after time, the clipper plowed her way to the tops of mountains and then plummeted into valleys so cavernous it seemed impossible we would ever emerge.

For Dix the captain's quarters provided the driest and warmest refuge in a heaving world. She crawled onto my lap and refused to budge, her earlier infatuation with the crew and ship forgotten. Miraculously, my own sickness did not recur, and since my attempt at mobility only gained me an assortment of bruises, I, too, remained stationary as much as I could.

The crew did not have that option, however. For them there was little shelter from the cold rains, the stinging sleet, hail and snow. Daily they sloshed through flooded decks or shoveled them clear of heavy snow drifts. Aloft they pounded frozen sails into obedience until their hands bled, and they cursed the day they turned to the sea.

Why had they? What mysterious lure drew men like my brother and Joshua and thousands more like them to this terrible way of life? Not for the pittance of their wages, surely. Nor was it love for the sea alone. It had to be something else, some basic need to try themselves against nature's worst. It made me wonder.

On a foggy afternoon on the fifty-third day of our voyage,

Joshua reckoned Cape San Diego, just north of the strait, to lie dead ahead. The light, however, was fast fading. It would be suicidal to go on without visibility.

Reluctantly, Joshua ran the *Neptune's Car* off to leeward and hove her to under close-reefed topsails to wait out the night. The tension on board was thick. In spite of the cold I felt as though we were hovering at the mouth of Dante's *Inferno*.

"Wind's freshening, and the rain's turning to sleet and snow," Joshua fretted as he came below after the dog watch. "Just what I feared. If we wake up to a blizzard tomorrow it means standing off another whole day, at least. We've got to stem the tide at the right moment."

Uncannily, our luck held. Daylight showed us clearing skies and a favorable breeze. Joshua lost no time. Ordering all sails set, he pointed the *Neptune's Car* for the Strait of Le Mair. We passed through it in a single day.

March 14, 1855

My dear Mama and Papa, our latitude is 51° 36′. We have rounded Cape Horn! Of course, we have still to cope with the roaring forties, but I begin to be optimistic that we shall, after all, make it alive. In whatever life that is left to me I shall never recall these past days and nights without a shudder.

Joshua is very nonchalant about our brush with death. He is most jubilant, however, about our time. He claims it is the best and fastest rounding he has ever made, and that if we can keep up our speed we have a chance at the *Flying Cloud's* record run. She made San Francisco in eighty-nine days! My husband's insistence on carrying a full press of sail in the worst of storms amounts to dementia. Frankly, I shall be happy just to set foot on land again.

The crew has no chance to recover from their ordeal as we

are now short two men. One man, Sinbad, fell from the upper deck and suffered a severe head injury and broken bones. Our other patient is Mr. O'Keefe, who has pneumonia. Most all of the men have suffered some degree of frostbite and there are a wide variety of gashes and bruises. About the only thing we don't yet have is scurvy—but since our captain will not hear of stopping in Valparaiso for fresh food we may yet have that to look forward to. *He* says we'll be perfectly fine as long as we have enough rainwater and onions. So why do I lay awake at night dreaming of salads and fruits and medium-rare steaks? One lone pig survives out of all our livestock. I have lost all of my inhibitions about doing away with him, but Joshua puts me off. I suspect it has something to do with the old sailors' superstition about it bringing bad luck. Perhaps he will let me have it for my birthday!

Poor Dix has emerged from our experience quite woebe-gone. A bit of sunlight and warmth would do us all some good—the temperatures have not risen above freezing for weeks.

I do wonder how you are all faring at home, whether Victoria has had her baby yet and whether either of my bachelor brothers are thinking of changing their ways. Do you hear from Andrew? Are you all well, and have you seen any crocuses yet? How I long for news!

Remember to keep this daughter of Neptune in your thoughts, as you ever remain in mine.

Your loving,
Mary.

As master of his little dominion, Joshua, I was coming to learn, was expected to be navigator, clergyman, officer of the law, trader, and physician. It had never once occurred to me, however, that I would be expected to act as nurse. When I ventured onto the deck for my first breath of fresh air in a fortnight he swooped down on me. Why, he wanted to know in his usual highhanded manner, was I not making myself useful in the sick bay?

"Impossible," I declared, recoiling. "I wouldn't be any use at all."

"Why not? I thought nursing was a natural instinct for women. Isn't Florence Nightingale one of your heroines?"

"I'm not Florence Nightingale."

"That's too bad. There are two men who require your tender ministrations. One of them is Mr. O'Keefe, the handsome lad with the smiling Irish eyes."

I flushed.

"Since you won't volunteer your services I shall have to require them," he said.

"What can I do that anyone else can't do?"

"That's exactly the point—I can't spare anyone else. I'm already shorthanded."

"So! I'm the only nonessential person on this ship. Very well, captain. I shall try to make myself more *useful*."

I marched below. I stopped to change into a more becoming dress and rearranged my hair and then went on to the sick bay. At first glance both patients appeared to be unconscious. The sailor assigned to keep an eye on them, however, assured me that Mr. O'Keefe was only asleep.

"It's Sinbad what caught it worst, poor bloke. Nearly split 'is skull in two. Wouldn't be 'alf surprise if 'e slips 'is cable, 'e's lost that much blood."

With that encouraging report the man departed. I stood there rather uncertainly, then approached the berth of the man they called Sinbad. My stomach turned over. An effort had been made to clean the blood from the terrible head wound, but some had clotted and dried in the thick dark hair.

Under a normally swarthy complexion the man's face held a deathly pallor. His breathing was deep and sighing. I swallowed.

"Glory be! Is it the mistress I'm lookin' at, or have I died and gone to heaven?"

"Mr. O'Keefe!" With relief I turned toward the second mate, who looked, by contrast, ruddily healthy. On closer inspection, however, I noticed that the color staining his cheeks was a little too hectic, the eyes too fever-bright.

"It is only myself, sir. The captain has sent me to help you and Sinbad get well again."

The second mate was suddenly convulsed by a violent fit of coughing. I watched in distress and then spotted Joshua's book, *The Sailor's Guide to Health*, on the table beside the medicine chest. Hurriedly I found the place dealing with pneumonia.

I read: *Flaxseed poultices, using flannel to envelop the entire chest, give relief and exercise a very beneficial influence on the inflammation of the lungs. Should the cough be dry and troublesome, three to five drops of tincture or extract of lobelia may be given every two hours in tea.*

I rummaged through the medicines and located a vial of extract of lobelia. At least, I thought, I could give Mr. O'Keefe the tea. Perhaps I could even manage the poultice with Manolo's help. I had seen Mama prepare them for chest colds.

Feeling better, I turned to the page on fractures. The *Guide* warned sternly: *The treatment of injuries received from the fracture of bones should never be attempted by the inexperienced.* Oh, dear. Poor Sinbad. I would have to try simply to keep him comfortable, and hope the head wound would heal by itself. What else was there to do?

I plunged with dedication into my new responsibilities. There was a certain nobility in laying a cool cloth upon the fevered brow that appealed to me. I was also conscious of the Irishman's keen attention; his eyes followed me with an expression that would flatter any woman. Why did Joshua never look at me like that?

But my husband was obviously more interested in following the movements of the *Westward Ho*. He and Mr. Buckley speculated at tedious length where she might be, the concensus being that the clipper was reaching for winds to our west. Joshua held the *Neptune's Car* closer to the coast. Either way it was a gamble. The fickle winds that sped one ship on her way might choose to leave another becalmed only forty or fifty miles distant.

It was a glad day for everyone when the roaring forties were left behind. Our heavy storm canvas was exchanged for lighter sail, and we skimmed up the western coast of South America with the southeast tradewinds at our back. Spirits were high.

Even my patients seemed to respond to the warmer latitudes. Sinbad's restlessness eased and Mr. O'Keefe improved visibly with each day. I assiduously plied him with broths and beef teas, taking an obscure pleasure in annoying Joshua who complained that I was neglecting my other duties. Finally Mr. Buckley ordered the second mate back to his work.

"You can't do that! Mr. O'Keefe is still weak," I protested.

"Aye, weak in the head, maybe. Fit enough to stand a watch."

Joshua, naturally, took his side. "It's Mr. Buckley's decision, Mary, and not my job to interfere." When I muttered rebelliously under my breath his eyebrows arched with mock surprise.

"Such concern! I think Miss Nightingale must have had an influence on you after all, my dear. Or was it Mr. O'Keefe?"

With only one patient left in my care I decided I had earned the right to some leisure. I basked in the sunshine with Dix, watching whoever was on duty measure our speed. It was a simple process: one man watched the time while another threw a log line over the side and counted the number of knots run out in a half minute. In three consecutive days during that period we averaged sixteen knots, covering 310, 310 and 313 miles, which everyone considered remarkable.

Dix amused herself between naps by pouncing on flying fish that stranded themselves on the deck. When Doc fried up a number for the captain's table I was surprised to find them quite delicious. Fish of all kinds, in fact, were plentiful and a welcome change from our diet which was now mostly dried, salted or tinned. The only thing that was not plentiful was water. As days went by without rain to replenish our supply Joshua became concerned. We were ordered to ration ourselves more carefully.

On her seventy-ninth day from New York the *Neptune's Car* crossed the equator for the second time. This was extraordinary time by anyone's standards and Joshua and the crew were beside themselves. I was able to persuade him it was the proper moment to kill the fatted pig.

"Is not good, señora. Bad luck will come," Manolo prophesied darkly.

"Nonsense!" I returned.

But two days after the pig died, our faithful companion the wind deserted us. We were becalmed.

chapter
9

Day after day, day after day
We stuck, nor breath nor motion;
As idle as a painted ship
Upon a painted ocean.

April 8, 1855

My dear sister, do you remember that long, gruesome poem we had to study in school, *The Rime of the Ancient Mariner*? Well, experiencing it is even worse than reading it. As I write this letter the *Neptune's Car* is stuck, quite literally, in the middle of the Pacific. And nothing can rescue us but the wind.

We have been here four dreadful days. The heat is even more intense than I remember it being on the Atlantic side. Water is short, and so are tempers. A fight erupted near the scuttlebut this afternoon, which Mr. O'Keefe promptly halted by striking both men with a belaying pin. Fortunately, no broken bones!

Joshua and I have our own troubles. Yesterday about midday a sudden squall broke over the ship. The rain pelted down and you have no idea how wonderful it felt—but do you think Joshua would allow me to enjoy it? No! I was ordered below to the unendurable heat of our cabin, just so the crew could stop up the scuppers and frolic naked on the flooded decks!

After five minutes of listening to their gleeful shouts I decided I had had enough. When Joshua came below I was soaking in an entire day's water ration in my copper hip bath.

If I were one of the crew I would have been strung to the yardarms at once. I'm not sure that wouldn't have been preferable to the tongue-lashing he gave me; he made it quite clear what he thought of his willful and disobedient wife. But oh, Victoria, that bath was worth every minute of it!

April 11. We are still becalmed. Sinbad, the man who was so badly injured and who has been my charge these weeks, worsened during the night, and died early this morning.

Joshua believes it was infection that killed him, aggravated by the heat. He says there was nothing we could have done. But somehow that doesn't help. A man was alive, and now he is dead.

A few hours ago there was a ceremony and Sinbad was committed to the sea. Dear Victoria, I cannot describe to you the horror of it, watching the water close over him—no grave, no stone to mark it, nothing. And there were sharks, Victoria. I know there were.

Afterward I went down to the cabin. I couldn't stop shaking. Joshua came and took me in his arms and told me I shouldn't cry for Sinbad, but he didn't understand. I was afraid of the sea, of death itself.

He tried to tell me that it doesn't matter what happens to the body after death. It is the spirit—our inner self—that is

important, he says. The spirit lives on for eternity. He
sounded so confident! I asked him how he could be certain
about such things and he replied that he had read about them
in the book God gave to man. I suppose he means the Bible.
Joshua has such a peculiar way of talking about God. And he
talks *to* him the same way—as though he were a regular
person. It makes me uncomfortable.

We have drifted for seven days now. The crew has given up
all their splendid hopes for a record. Mr. Buckley claims we
might still best the *Westward Ho* if she ran into calms. . . .
Joshua says nothing at all.

Oh, I do hate sailing ships!

Late the following day we heard the sounds we had all been
waiting for: the faint stirring of canvas, the creak of timber,
the slap of rigging against spars. We lifted our eyes, hardly
daring to hope. And then we saw the sails lift, slacken again,
and then fill. The ship began to move. A cry rang out, and
men sprang to brace the yards. The *Neptune's Car* began the
final lap to California.

With the release of tension there was almost a holiday
atmosphere aboard the clipper. Men pitched in with a will to
make ready for port. This meant scraping down all the
woodwork and applying two or three coats of paint, tarring
the rigging, rubbing down the brass, and, of course, holy-
stoning the deck planks to a spotless white. According to
Joshua, a vessel was expected to sail into port as proudly as
she sailed out.

Unfortunately, we were not sailing into the same port that
we had sailed out of; Boston was now a continent's span
away. The prospect of going ashore anywhere at all, however,
was enough to send my spirits soaring. I spent hours going

over my wardrobe, deliberating what to wear. Would California ladies wear different fashions from Boston ladies? I applied to Joshua, who said dryly there were hardly any "ladies" at all in California, unless one included the uninhibited members of our sex who frequented the saloons. And they wore very little at all!

Several outward bound ships hove into view, dipping their colors. We might have gotten fresh fruits and vegetables from them but Joshua would stop for nothing now. All sights were set on the Golden Gate.

Early on the morning of April 25, 1855, I rose and dressed with particular care. On this day, after one hundred and one days and fifteen thousand miles at sea, we would reach the end of our voyage.

I was just putting the final touches on my costume when I heard the welcome cry, "*Land ho!*" An instant later I was at the rail, seeing it for myself. The South Farallon Islands were close at hand, meaning that we were only twenty-five miles from our destination.

I could hardly contain my excitement. "The first thing I'm going to do when we get ashore is have a big juicy steak an inch thick, and a crisp Waldorf salad! No, first I want a bath, in gallons and gallons of fresh water."

Joshua laughed. "I promise you the biggest bath and the thickest steak in San Francisco."

"Really?"

"Really. We'll go to all the finest restaurants. A different one every night, if you like!"

A brisk wind, a cloudless sky and dancing blue waters provided the perfect backdrop as the *Neptune's Car* raced for the finish. At the Heads we paused momentarily to take on a pilot, and then, "shipshape and Bristol fashion," we waltzed grandly into San Francisco Bay.

The crew jumped into the rigging to furl sails for the last time. I glanced at Joshua. What was he feeling now, I wondered. Pride? Satisfaction that he had kept—and bettered—his promise to the owners? The expression on his face gave me a jolt.

"Joshua, what is it?"

He nodded grimly toward one of the piers where a large, majestic-looking clipper was being unloaded. We were passing close enough for me to make out the golden nameplate on her stern: The *Westward Ho*.

"I'm sorry, Joshua," I whispered. "I really am."

He turned to the pilot. "When did that clipper make port?"

"The *Westward Ho*, sir? Just last evenin'. And a fine passage it was, too, sir. Nigh on one-hundred-one days from Boston."

I saw Joshua's eyes flicker. He said, slowly, "I wonder how that compares to a ship that sailed a day later, from New York?"

The pilot whistled. "Sounds to me, sir, like you've run a mighty close race! In fact—"

"In fact, we might've just took the blue ribbon after all!" Mr. Buckley broke in exultantly.

"The experts will have to decide that. However, I would say Captain Hussey might be advised to postpone his victory celebration!"

The *Neptune's Car* was brought up smoothly alongside Market Wharf, and the small crowd that had gathered cheered their admiration. All hands moved hastily to complete the final duties. And then, at last, they were free.

I watched with amazement as a bevy of shouting, gesticulating men closed around the sailors as soon as their feet touched the wharf.

"Boardinghouse runners," Joshua told me. "All offering free liquor and tobacco in exchange for their patronage. Nine-tenths of the men will be half-shot within the hour."

I thought of my brother Andrew. "And shanghaied?"

"Probably not. Fortunately that isn't as common as it was."

It seemed to take forever for Joshua to go through the formalities and turn the ship's manifest over to the agent. Finally he offered to escort me to the hotel.

How odd and wonderful to feel the earth once more beneath my feet! My senses reeled at the noises, the colors, the vibrant mass of humanity that surged through the crowded streets. They threatened to overpower me. *So this,* I thought, *is the City of Gold!* It was not what I had pictured it to be.

"Hard to believe this place was only a hamlet before the gold rush," said Joshua. "Now there must be close to fifty thousand people, and bursting at the seams."

That was apparent. Some of the buildings looked as though they had been nailed together overnight.

"It's not exactly Boston, is it?"

"It doesn't try to be. It has its own attraction. There's a spirit of adventure in Frisco I find infectious. People aren't set in their ways."

I was both disappointed and relieved to reach the hotel. Then I forgot my disappointment in delighted awe at the extravagant plush carpets and glittering chandeliers. We followed a smartly dressed bellhop to our suite, where I rounded on Joshua suspiciously.

"I thought your salary was only fifty dollars a month."

"Plus a percentage of the freight profits. And don't forget the bonus Foster and Nickerson promised if we made port in a hundred and three days or better."

"We're rich!" I clasped my hands in anticipation.

"Temporarily. I intend to reinvest most of our profits in shares of the *Neptune's Car.* But as long as we're in the City of Gold, we may as well live in style."

He reached for me but I held him off.

"Have you made up your mind, yet—about sending me home?"

"You want to know now? We've scarcely arrived!"

"Please, Joshua."

"Very well." His voice was cold. "I have decided that you will stay with me, where you belong. Your home is the *Neptune's Car*."

"*Never!* I will never consider that ship my home! I hate it."

"And me? Do you hate me also, Mary?"

"I—I don't know! Maybe our marriage was a mistake. Maybe I was too young," I said, tears of frustration filling my eyes. "Joshua, why can't you admit it? I'm not cut out to be a captain's wife!"

"There's no point in discussing this." He picked up the cap he had flung down. "My mind is made up. I'm going back to the ship. When I return we'll go out and see the town."

I let him go without a reply. Why, why did he have to be so stubborn? It was pride, it had to be—the same pride that kept him from admitting defeat in a race with another ship.

A knock interrupted my angry reflections. Would Mrs. Patten care for her bath now? Captain Patten had ordered hot water sent up.

As I took a long, lovely soak in the scented water another thought occurred to me. If we had lost the race with the *Westward Ho* Joshua might find it difficult—even impossible—to secure another charter. We would *have* to return home again!

By the time Joshua came to collect me I had regained my composure, convinced that things would work out.

"I'm pleased that you've decided to be sensible." Joshua's eyes traveled approvingly over my fashionable lilac-and-cream gown. "The rest of the day is at your disposal, fair lady. What would you like to see?"

"Everything! I'll go anywhere there's people. And I want to go to one of those fancy restaurants you promised me!"

San Francisco was as fascinating as Joshua said it was. There was a rawness about the city—not surprising since it had been rebuilt twice after disastrous fires. But even the inhabitants were unique. Strolling through Portsmouth Square we spotted red-shirted miners mixing with elegant Mexican landowners in velvet embroidered jackets. I gaped at a gambler who I was sure was wearing a diamond-studded vest, and Joshua pointed out robed Chinese, their long queues dangling down their backs.

The only persons who did not seem very much in evidence were women. But that was changing, Joshua explained. The Vigilance Committee was clamping down on the rampant thefts, murders and lynching parties of a few years before. The city boasted a new respectability, and many men were now sending for their wives and children.

When we grew tired of walking Joshua hired a carriage and we drove out to the Presidio, then south along the beach path to Lake Merced where we stopped for supper. The menu at the Lake House fulfilled all of my dearest longings. I ate my way through five courses while Joshua predicted I would make myself sick. I didn't, but I fell asleep on the way back to the city and he put me to bed like a child when we reached the hotel. For the first time in months I slept without being rocked by the sea.

The next morning, going to the dining room, the desk clerk stopped us. He was waving a copy of the *Golden Era*.

"Have you read the newspaper, sir? They're saying you may have won the race!"

My heart stopped. Joshua took the paper and scanned through the article on the front page. Then he read it aloud:

The city of San Francisco hails the arrival of two heroic clippers, the *Westward Ho* and *Neptune's Car,* that made their dash around the perilous Cape Horn in the closest race of the season. So close, in fact, that even the experts have not yet named the winner! While it is true that Captain Hussey cleared the Golden Gate with his ship, the *Westward Ho,* a day ahead of her rival, he also had the advantage of a day's head start from Boston. Captain Patten of the gallant *Neptune's Car* departed New York port on January 14. He was only 54 days to the Horn and docked here yesterday after one hundred and one days.

Whatever the outcome, congratulations are most certainly deserved by both masters for the smartest sailing of the season. The *Era* looks forward to reporting the winner of the race as soon as the debate is settled.

"Did you hear that?" Joshua sang out. "We've won! It's almost a certainty."

"I don't see how you can say that. Captain Hussey had a head start, but he also had farther to go."

Joshua brushed that aside. "Those paltry few miles between Boston and New York are hardly worth considering."

He was obviously in no mood for clear-headed logic and departed for his ship after a hearty breakfast. For the next several days his time would be occupied in superintending the off-loading and sale of our cargo. He would also, I knew, be searching for another commission, the sooner the better, since every idle day meant a loss to the shipowners.

My own time was to be filled more pleasurably. Since Joshua refused to allow me to venture off on my own, I introduced myself to another of the hotel's residents, a Mrs. Thomas, and together we sallied forth happily to shop.

The stalls of San Francisco were as exotic as those of a

foreign country. Here were none of the neatly cobbled lanes and dignified storefronts of Boston. Shop space was so inadequate that goods tumbled untidily onto the sidewalks, under awnings or makeshift canopies. Pedestrians were often compelled to thread their way through the narrow streets one at a time.

My companion informed me that the thoroughfares were also used as meeting places. Indeed, we observed a number of groups, especially on Montgomery Street, gathered in heated discussions. Passing close to one such group I chanced to overhear the names "Patten" and *"Neptune's Car,"* and tugged on Mrs. Thomas's sleeve.

"They're talking about the race!" I hissed. "Let's stop."

"We can't do that," she said, looking horrified. "Our motive for loitering might be . . . mistaken! What if we were taken for Ladies of Ill Repute?"

I looked at Mrs. Thomas's stout form and stifled a giggle. With an effort to appear nonchalant we strolled on.

By the time we returned to the hotel we were both laden with parcels. Joshua would be cross, I reflected, holding a new shirtwaist against me before a mirror to study the effect, but surely I was entitled to some recompense for all the misery I'd suffered? When he finally came in I was stretched out on a chaise lounge nibbling vanilla drops and enthralled in new a novel.

"Well, I don't need to ask if you've had a good day."

"I knew you'd be upset, and I only bought a fraction of the things Mrs. Thomas bought. A shirtwaist or two, cloth to make you a vest, thread and ribbons and—"

"Sweets? I'll bet you've gained at least five pounds since we arrived."

"Well! What's put you in such a foul mood?"

"We lost. That's what." He threw himself into a chair.

"The *race?*"

"The official time for the *Neptune's Car* was one hundred days, twenty-three and a half hours. The *Westward Ho,* one hundred days, eighteen hours."

"Only five and a half hours difference!"

He ran an exasperated hand through his hair. "It may as well have been a week."

"Why is being first so terribly important?" I cried. "Everyone says you sailed well. You would have set a new record it it weren't for those eight days of calms!"

" 'Would have' and 'almost' doesn't count, Mary, not in anyone's book. You heard the owners back in New York. The first vessel into port is the first to get another charter."

"So you think—we might not get one?"

Disastrously, I allowed hope to creep into my voice. His jaw tightened.

"We won't be running back to Boston with our tail between our legs, if that's what you had in mind! I'll sail to China in ballast first."

As suddenly as the anger had come it vanished. He looked tired.

"Get dressed, Mary. We'll take supper downstairs to-night."

For the next two weeks neither of us mentioned the race. Joshua attended to business, taking an occasional afternoon or evening off to show me around town. One Sunday we wandered to the top of Telegraph Hill for a dazzling view of the bay and to sip the famous milk punch served at the station. Another time we joined the promenade along the beach to Point San José. I delighted in every new thing, unconsciously storing away memories against the long, dreary hours at sea that were soon to come.

Mail day came at last, and I wept and laughed my way through the stack of letters from home. How strange it was to be reading of events that were now just history to the writer. Victoria's baby was born, a sweet girl named Gwendolyn. Papa and George wanted to know what San Francisco was really like; Mama only hoped that I was happy. I read each letter over until I had committed them to memory. Then I posted long letters in return. Where would I be when they received them?

I was not long in finding out. While dining together one night at the Sans Souci House, Joshua announced abruptly he had contracted a cargo for China. I choked on my Coquilles St. Jacques.

"Why did you have to tell me now and ruin everything?"

"You mean your appetite has been spoiled? I didn't think it was possible! Forgive me, my dear."

"What kind of cargo is it?"

"Cotton and lumber, nothing unusual. Did I ever tell you about the captain I knew who shipped a hundred dead Chinese? He listed them as passengers and charged the relatives seventy-five dollars each!"

"What a revolting story," I said, stabbing angrily at my broccoli. I noticed a heavy-set man in a captain's brass-buttoned coat wending his way toward us. He stopped by the table and removed the cigar from his mouth.

"Captain Patten?"

"Aye. I'm Captain Patten."

"Glad to make your acquaintance, sir." He thrust out his hand. "I'm Hussey of the *Westward Ho.*"

"What an unexpected pleasure. Allow me to introduce my wife."

"Ma'am?" He gave me a perfunctory bow and turned his attention back to Joshua. "That wasn't a bad performance you gave, son. Even had me worried once or twice. Your first command, I understand."

"That's right." Joshua's voice was curt.

"Well, it takes time to get the feel of a ship. Don't take it too hard, Patten. Ain't a clipper built that can out-sail the *Westward Ho.*"

"I marvel at your confidence, sir, after winning by so narrow a margin."

Hussey stiffened. He jammed the cigar back between his teeth. I was aware of the hush that had fallen over the tables near us. Whatever transpired now would be telegraphed through the streets of San Francisco by daylight.

"It's in the wind that you're chartered for Hong Kong, Captain Patten. Happens I'm heading that way myself. You wouldn't care to settle the question once and for all?"

Joshua smiled. The entire assembly of diners held their breath. All but me, of course. I already knew what his answer would be.

"Captain Hussey, sir. . . . I would be delighted."

The hush was broken by a babble of excited voices, clapping and cheers. The two men shook hands, then the master of the *Westward Ho* threaded his way back to a rowdy group of friends. I watched Hussey lift his glass with a triumphant smirk.

"Now you've gone and done it, Joshua Patten! You and your pride."

The *Neptune's* reputation was at stake. I had no choice."

"So it was her reputation you were thinking of?" I said sarcastically, and he grinned.

"Not entirely."

Our last days in California speeded by. On the twelfth of May the hold of the *Neptune's Car* was loaded, and that evening I stood once more upon her afterdeck, watching the light of the city's numberless gaslights gleaming upon the bay.

"What are you thinking?" asked the man beside me.

"I'm wishing this was a summer night at home, and those were the lights of Boston Bay."

"I shouldn't have asked."

"No. I don't suppose there is anything that would make you reconsider letting me go home?"

To my surprise, there was a hesitation. "Only one thing. But it doesn't signify in your case."

"What? Tell me."

"If you were with child I would consent to return you to your family. I would put you on the steamer myself."

I was dumbfounded.

"I know what you're thinking. Other women in their term have sailed, they've even given birth aboard. But to me it's a risk. I wouldn't take that risk with our child."

My face fell. It was the child he was thinking about.

I said, "If that's what it takes, then I will pray night and day for one!"

Joshua did not reply and I turned and walked below.

chapter 10

The *Neptune's Car* weighed anchor at first light. The crew looked even sorrier than the lot we shipped out with from New York, but Mr. Buckley said we were lucky. During the gold rush days boarding house crimps would even pass off dead men as drunken sailors, filling their clothing with straw and inserting a few rats to provide motion!

Sailing ships, I had learned, changed crews frequently in order not to pay their wages while in port. Unfortunately this custom did not always apply to the officers. I would still have to contend with the disagreeable Mr. Buckley, and the cook had signed on for another voyage. Mr. O'Keefe had not; I wondered suspiciously if Joshua had had anything to do with that. What disappointed me most was Manolo's failure to turn up. Joshua had waited until the last minute and then replaced him with an efficient Oriental named Ling Wu.

"Couldn't trust that Mexicano, anyway," Mr. Buckley declared with his usual disregard for accuracy.

"Manolo was from Chile."

"Don't matter, they're all the same." We glared at each other, our animosity rekindled.

The only one that had welcomed me aboard with any degree of enthusiasm was Dix. She twined around my skirts, purring full throttle; but any illusions of my being essential to her well-being were flattened when she dashed away to ingratiate herself with the new second mate.

A number of the hands were Sandwich Islanders, called Kanakas, with friendly bronzed faces and flashing smiles. I asked Joshua if we would be stopping at the Sandwich Islands.

"Can't risk it," he said. "They'd jump ship and I'd lose a crew. We may send a boat in for fruit if we have time."

Little chance, I thought gloomily.

For our first ten days after setting sail we were plagued by strong westerly winds, which meant we had to drive into the wind's eye. After two days I could repeat the tacking orders by heart:

"*Haul up crossjack and mainsails!*" Joshua gave this instruction after stationing himself by the helmsman. Then he would cry,

"*Ready about!*" sending the hands scurrying around to clear away any cordage that might prevent the yards from swinging freely.

"*Down helm!*" came next, and the helmsman spun his wheel in the direction of the wind. I didn't like this part, because as the *Neptune's Car* swung across the wind, her sails were taken aback and she trembled violently. If the wind happened to shift at this delicate point we were in trouble, for the canvas was sitting on the wrong side of the masts.

Finally, at precisely the right moment, Joshua shouted, "*Let go and haul!*" and the crew worked furiously to reset the crossjack and mainsails in double time.

Mr. Buckley said the maneuver was never directed by anyone but the captain, but I thought this rather exaggerated his importance. It didn't look all that difficult.

The whole first week we kept pace with the *Westward Ho,* which was having its own problems with the wind. Not many people actually see a clipper with every sail set and drawing. Even I had to admit she made an impressive sight. As we slipped further south into the variables of Cancer we moved further apart, and it was in this latitude we saw the corposant.

The light breeze of the afternoon had died away, leaving us with the hot breathlessness that usually meant a thunder-storm. When I went on deck after supper to seek relief from the heat, the hands were already aloft clewing up sail. I watched idly from my deck chair.

Suddenly I sat up straight. "Joshua. What's that light— high in the main masthead?"

He came over to me. "It's a corposant. Sailors call it St. Elmo's fire."

"What is it? What causes it?"

"No one's really sure. A storm in the air, perhaps. . . . Seamen regard it as an omen."

"Of course! They think of everything as an omen. Is this one supposed to portend good or evil?"

"Good, if the light rises in the rigging. If it drops they'll say we're in for dirty weather."

For some minutes we watched the ghostly fire flicker from one to the other of the masts. The crew reacted with uncharacteristic nervousness, moving hastily to finish their work. Then one man looked up. Even from my position I could see the eerie glow cast upon the uplifted face. Joshua drew in his breath.

"What's wrong?"

"Sailors believe that the light of a corposant falling upon a man's face means certain death."

"What rubbish. Surely you don't believe that."

He did not answer, concentrating on the man who appeared to have frozen to the yardarm. Mr. Buckley reported aft.

"It's Manlias, sir, one of the lascars. Should I send a lad to bring him down?"

"No. He'll come down."

And so he did, a moment or two after that, tossing a laughing remark to his mates as his feet touched the deck. The corposant made one last appearance, dipping below the topmast crosstrees, and then disappeared.

"Well! He doesn't act like he considers himself doomed."

Joshua shrugged. "Perhaps not. But you don't spend years in a forecastle without understanding how a seaman thinks. And it's how we think that shapes how we will act in a crisis. We have more of a hand in our own destinies than we like to believe."

A few drops of rain pattered to the deck, accompanied by a grumble of thunder. I ran for shelter, although I would have liked to have stayed and argued. Joshua did make the most illogical statements!

Two days later the barometer plunged and kept falling, lower than I had ever seen it. The sky, though clear, was leaden, the sea rolling in thick swells. I had an uneasy feeling in the pit of my stomach and went to find out from Joshua what it was all about.

The scene on deck was not heartening. Orders were flying right and left. The off-duty watch had been called out, and all hands were engaged in sending down studding booms, royal and topgallant yards. I realized very suddenly that I had never before seen them do this—not even at the Horn. Joshua confirmed the worst with a single word. *Typhoon.*

When all is said and done, there is pitifully little that a ship can do to prepare for nature's most terrible assaults. Sails are useless, so they are removed. Towering masts are a hazard, snapped off like twigs on a tree. A vessel's hope lies in her buoyancy, and her freedom to run clear of land.

Aboard the *Neptune's Car* I worked frantically to put away every moveable object. Last of all I lashed myself into my berth and laid there, listening, until at last I heard the roaring sound that made my blood run cold. With all the power and fury of a locomotive, the typhoon rammed into the *Neptune's Car.*

How long it was before I suddenly remembered Dix I cannot say. I recalled, fearfully, that I had last seen her in the saloon and that Ling Wu, unlike Manolo, would not take care to see that she was shut up safely below. What if she was in the next room, trying to find me?

I untied the lashings and got up, grabbing at the corner of a bureau to steady myself, then lurched from one piece of furniture to the next. At the saloon door I wrenched open the handle and fell into the darkness.

"Dix!" My cry was drowned by the rushing wind, and I saw that at the far end of the room the weather door to the main deck had blown open. Floods of water were washing down the steps. Could she have escaped that way?

"Dix, where are you?" I advanced a few more staggering steps, groping for support. Then I slipped. My head struck the table as I went down.

For three long days the *Neptune's Car* struggled for survival. Finally the typhoon tired of its cruel game and moved away, tossing the ship aside like a broken toy. When I went on deck, still nursing bruised ribs and a lump on my head, Joshua pointed out the damages: the broken fore and mizzen masts that had brought down with them a tangle of rigging; the badly sprung mainmast; the longboats smashed beyond repair; the missing rails and livestock.

"It's a wonder we survived," I murmured, and caught a flash of pain on Joshua's face before he turned it away.

"Not everyone did. We lost a man, Mary. There wasn't a chance of lowering a boat."

Manlias. I knew without asking, before he told me what I did not want to hear.

"That poor man . . . I'm so sorry, Joshua."

There was another loss, one that was not deeply mourned by anyone but me. I searched the ship from bow to stern before I would accept it. My companion and playmate, Dix, had disappeared without a trace.

The *Neptune's Car* was in urgent need of repairs. We had been blown hundreds of miles off course, and the decision had to be made whether to put in at one of the uncharted South Sea Islands, or do what we could at sea and proceed under jury-rig to the Sandwich Islands. Joshua chose the latter. The crew cleared away the wreckage, and we limped slowly on our way.

The fate of the *Westward Ho* was on all our minds. Had she survived the typhoon? Or had she, by some freak turn of nature, escaped it entirely? There was still no sign of her when our anchor rattled into the turquoise waters of Oahu.

I fell instantly in love with the islands. The natives crowded around happily, offering fragrant garlands of hibiscus and baskets of fruit. The people of the English-speaking community invited us into their homes. Unfortunately, most of the hospitality was wasted on Joshua. He labored night and day overseeing the repairs on his ship and was greatly exasperated when the Kanakas did not exhibit the same dedication. I did my best, however, to make up for his ungracious behavior. Each day I sallied forth for teas and carriage rides and elaborate dinners, admiring (without much effort) everyone and everything in that lush tropical paradise.

After almost a week Joshua set himself to rounding up another crew, since most of the original members had vanished into the vegetation. Then the *Westward Ho* finally put in to port. She was in an even worse state than we had been, leaking badly. But she had, at least, survived.

On the day we weighed anchor, the *Neptune's Car* dipped her colors—once to the well-wishers on shore, and once to our rival as we passed by. Joshua was whistling, looking rather smug.

"Doesn't the Bible say something about being glad at your neighbor's calamity?" I asked pointedly.

He lifted his eyebrows. "You don't think I'd want Captain Hussey and his crew in Davy Jones' locker? Then we'd have to call off the race!"

chapter
11

Happily, we met with no further disasters during the three week passage to the China Sea. A half-thousand nautical miles from Hong Kong I saw my first junk, and boats appeared after that with frequency. One of them made as if to approach. I waved them closer in an encouraging fashion until I noticed the mate waving them away with a gun.

"Mr. Buckley, really, is that necessary? Surely you aren't afraid of innocent fishermen?"

"Those 'innocent fishermen,' as you call them, are more than likely pirates who would as soon slit your throat as look at you."

"Pirates!" My jaw fell open.

"Yes, ma'am. These waters is crawlin' with 'em."

"You can't be serious. Joshua, he isn't serious, is he?"

"I'm afraid Mr. Buckley is right, Mary."

"You mean to say we've crossed these thousands of miles and survived the heat and ice and that wretched typhoon just to fall into the hands of bloodthirsty heathens?"

"Never fear, my love. Our cargo is too valuable for me to let that happen."

"Cargo, indeed!" I sputtered.

By the time the green coastal mountains were defined on the horizon the waters were thick with traffic. Joshua ordered frequent soundings, wary of the many uncharted reefs and shoals. At the mouth of the Tathong Channel we picked up a pilot and were soon entering the busy harbor of Hong Kong.

China! It seemed incredible that I should be gazing at the mysterious and exotic spectacle that now confronted me. Beside the conventional barks and schooners anchored in the harbor moved a host of miscellaneous craft that Joshua identified as tankas, lorchas, and egg-boats. Dozens of these were already bobbing around the *Neptune's Car,* their owners vying for attention, shouting in a curious hybrid of Chinese and English.

"You see how easy it is to do your marketing in China," Joshua gestured. You don't have to go to the stalls, they come to you. Boat people will sell you anything you want. Including themselves."

I sucked in my breath, horrified.

As our ship drew alongside one of the rambling company warehouses that lined the waterfront, a blast of unpleasant odors assaulted my nostrils. I reached hastily for my handkerchief.

"I thought you told me 'Hong Kong' meant 'Fragrant Streams.' "

He laughed. "Better get used to it. We'll be here for a while."

"What do you mean, a *while?* How long does it take to load a cargo of tea?"

"Loading isn't the problem, it's finding the tea. That typhoon set us back. I'd counted on getting here in time for the early crop. There's no chance of that, now."

"Well, you've won the race, at least. That should count in

your favor. Captain Hussey won't make port for another week or two."

In actual fact the *Westward Ho* did not creep into port until eleven days later. But by then we were in no mood for jubilation. Joshua had been informed there was absolutely no chance of securing a cargo for months. We would have to bide our time at least through the terrible monsoon season of July and August, and possibly September as well.

"I can't endure it!" I wailed, when he told me. "Two months in this horrible climate and my health will be a shambles! I feel sick already."

"That's because you eat too much. You have to get accustomed to the native food."

"Would you take away my only consolation? Besides, I'm sure it's something else. I just feel so nauseated when I wake up."

For once, Joshua seemed to hear what I was saying. "If you want to see a doctor I'll get one."

"Tomorrow?"

"Very well."

The rotund little physician, however, was irritatingly cheerful. He listened unsympathetically to my complaints and then pronounced me a healthy young woman—"aside from the slight disorder of the digestion. Easy to pick up here. One has to be a bit careful."

Joshua came in just as he was departing.

"Everything all right?"

"Oh, yes," I said bitterly. "Nothing that a few months won't cure." The doctor clapped him on the back. "Not to worry, captain. One of nature's little surprises. Just take care and watch the diet."

He left. Joshua, looking dazed, sat on the bed and took my hand.

"So it's true. That's why you're gaining weight."

I didn't catch his meaning. Unhappily, I replied, "By the end of August I'll look like a cow."

"There's bound to be a berth available on one of the passenger schooners leaving for the States. I'll make inquiries right away."

I gaped. It now occurred to me that Joshua had leaped to the wrong conclusion. I had to set him right.

"Joshua—"

"Not now. You're tired. We'll talk more later."

I sat up. "I'm perfectly all right! Listen to me, Joshua. The doctor didn't mean that I—"

"I know exactly what he meant." He pressed me firmly back on the pillows. "But we're not taking any chances. Not with my son! Just lie there quietly for a change."

Perspiration beaded my forehead. *This is absurd,* I told myself. *Tell him the truth, now, before he goes and books you a passage home. But why should you?* Another voice inside me whispered, *All you have to do is let him go. Don't say a word. What right does he have to keep you here against your will?*

It was too easy to remain silent. Within a few days Joshua had secured a cabin for me in a schooner soon to leave Hong Kong for New York. The hard part was sustaining the deception. Joshua made things worse by being unusually considerate, supplying me with specially prepared foods and insisting that I take home generous gifts for everyone in the family. He himself chose toys for my little niece and nephew.

"Look at this teak boat, Mary," he said one day as we walked by a woodcarver's stall. "Looks something like the *Neptune's Car,* doesn't it? Let's buy it."

I swished flies away with my handkerchief. "We have enough presents. Victoria and Robert will complain we're spoiling their children."

"Then we'll keep it for our son."

I groaned and closed my eyes.

"Mary, what is it?"

"Nothing."

"There is. Take my arm, we'll find a rickshaw."

We were soon on our way back to the ship.

"I wish you'd stop fussing over me, Joshua! I'm all right. It's just that you—"

"I what, my dear?"

"You keep talking about a son! What if there is no son, Joshua?"

"I'll be perfectly happy with a daughter."

"That isn't what I mean." I swallowed. "Heaven help me. You are going to hate me forever, but I must tell you. Joshua—there's not going to be any child at all."

He stared at me uncomprehendingly.

"It was all a misunderstanding. The doctor only said I had a minor digestive upset. But you believed what you wanted to believe. And I let you."

He was absolutely still.

"Try to understand, Joshua. It was the only way you'd let me go home!"

He looked at me directly, then, and I flinched at what I saw.

"I asked you once if you hated me. Now it seems I have my answer."

"It's not you I hate! It's this place! The ship!" A thought occurred to me and I clutched his arm. "You will still let me go? Please, Joshua."

There was no answer. I began to sob. "You want to punish me. You'll keep me here until I die from some hideous disease, or else pirates murder me in my bed."

Still no reply.

"I didn't have to tell you the truth! I could have boarded that boat in two days and let you go on believing I carried your child."

"Do you wish to be commended for your honesty?" he asked icily.

"You're not such a shining example of honesty! Why don't you admit the real reason why you've dragged me halfway around the world? Not for the pleasure of my company, certainly."

"What are you talking about?"

"This obsession you have for a son! *He's* the only reason you were willing to let me go home. It was only his safety you cared about! Well, Captain Patten, if it's a son that will buy my freedom, then I'll give you a son before I'm made to leave Boston a second time!"

He looked disgusted. "I begin to believe you haven't any natural instincts in you at all."

"Perhaps, sir, I haven't found the man to arouse them."

His face turned to stone.

"I had planned to sail tomorrow for Canton. I will leave as scheduled. Buckley can look after the *Neptune's Car*.

"What about me?"

"I will arrange for you to stay ashore with an English merchant family I know—the Moultons. I've been their guest several times in the past and they are anxious to meet you."

The Moultons, when we met the next day, made me feel welcome indeed, although they were keenly disappointed that Joshua had to leave immediately for Canton. Edna Moulton was a square, sturdily built woman of middle years who announced that she was delighted to have another woman to talk to. "Now that my boys are off to school in England I simply can't find enough to do in a day! I shall undertake to show you Hong Kong, my dear. I daresay I'm qualified after all these years, wouldn't you, Frederick?"

"Mm, what's that? Qualified? Of course, of course." He went back to a discussion of freight rates with Joshua.

"Dear Frederick. He hasn't a clue as to what I say most of the time. Never mind. The two of us will have a splendid go of it." She patted my hand. "We quite despaired of seeing Joshua married, you know. He never paid any attention to the girls in the colony, although they paid plenty of attention to him, even as a first officer. There was a story that went around about a girl back in New England who died of the influenza. But you know how these rumors get about! Probably not a word of truth in it. Anyway," she beamed, "we are simply enchanted to meet Joshua's lovely bride! And how brave of you, my dear, to follow your young captain to the ends of the earth!"

Joshua choked on his tea. I inquired hastily, "Have you lived in China for very long, ma'am?"

"Oh dear, yes. Forever, it seems, though not always in Hong Kong. The British have only had possession of the island since 1841. Or was it 1843, Frederick?"

"What's that, dear?"

"No matter. The important thing is that it's ours now."

Joshua unexpectedly directed his attention to us. "A lot of people wonder what will happen if the Chinese decide they want their land back."

She shuddered. "It doesn't bear thinking about. Does it, Frederick? It would be like the old days in Macao, the wives and children living together and the men miles away in Canton."

"Canton?"

"That's where all the foreign factories were, my dear. The Chinese permitted only businessmen to live there. No wives, not even servants. And no foreign ships were allowed to sail into Canton. All the loading and unloading had to be done thirteen miles downriver, at Whampoa. All frightfully inconvenient."

"I should think so," I said politely.

"Especially for the opium clippers. They had to discharge their cargo at Lintin Island, fifty miles from Canton, before it could be smuggled on barges the rest of the way."

"Opium? What is that you're saying about opium, Edna dear?"

Apparently Frederick Moulton had the gift of picking and choosing from his wife's conversation what he wanted to hear.

"I was speaking of opium clippers, love. How difficult the trading used to be."

"Still is. Pirates hereabouts have put rather a cramp on things."

Joshua scowled. "That's putting it mildly. There were seven hundred ships burned the last year I was here. The captain's a fool who will put his ship and crew at hazard carrying opium.

My eyes widened. "Then why do they do it?"

Laughter bubbled from Edna Moulton, and even her husband contributed a dry cough.

"My dear, forgive me, but you are so refreshingly naive!"

"It's the money, of course," grunted Frederick. "There's a fortune in opium. Illegal, but everybody wants the stuff and the mandarins will pay a king's ransom for it."

"My husband has just been trying to persuade Joshua to make a delivery up the coast. Only a short run. The risk would be minimal; and the profits—! You and Joshua could afford to run back to America in ballast, without all this tiresome shopping for another cargo!"

I gasped. "Joshua—"

"The Moultons were quite aware, even before they brought it up, that I would never entertain the idea."

"But why not, if it isn't dangerous?"

He gave me an impatient look.

"Your husband isn't afraid of pirates, Mary dear. Joshua has a quaint moralistic notion that opium is—well, unhealthy."

"Deadly is the word I would have chosen, Edna."

She laughed. "You see? He is quite impossible."

"But didn't you give me opium the time I had the heat stroke, Joshua? I remember how wonderful it was, like a miracle after the pain. Surely any drug can be deadly if it is overused."

"My point, exactly," affirmed our host. "Excess in consumption is to be deplored, naturally. The Chinese simply don't seem to know when to stop."

"They'd stop smoking the poison if we stopped supplying it."

"You Americans are so absurdly self-righteous about such matters. Where has your Prohibition gotten you?"

Joshua took a deep breath. "You have to make a start somewhere. If you saw strong men turn into skeletons, as I have, rotting slowly in those filthy dens—"

"Come, now, Patten," Mr. Moulton cleared his throat. "No point in painting an ugly picture for the ladies, is there?"

"No. No point at all." He got to his feet. "It's time I took my leave, sir. My lorcha is due to sail within the hour." He extended his hand. "Thank you again for consenting to look after Mary."

"We will take good care of her for you, my boy. No hard feelings, I hope? Best of luck in finding a cargo."

"Come along, Frederick. Let's give the children a few moments to themselves. Goodbye, my dear." She kissed Joshua. "You will take care, won't you?"

Tactfully they withdrew. Joshua strode over to a window and stared moodily out at the neatly tended gardens.

"You'll be comfortable here. The Moultons are well-to-do, as you have no doubt gathered, and they have a number of friends who should keep you amused."

"How long will you be gone?"

He shrugged. "Two, three weeks, maybe more. If I have no luck finding a charter in Canton I'll try the other open ports."

"Isn't it rather dangerous to go wandering about by yourself?"

"Contrary to the impression the Moultons may have given you, the Chinese are not all ignorant and bloodthirsty heathens lying in wait to slit the throat of every foreign devil that comes their way. The great majority of them are refined and courteous people. I enjoy dealing with them far more than I enjoy dealing with most of our own merchants."

There seemed to be nothing more to say.

"Well, then. I won't keep you. Goodbye, Joshua. Good luck."

He turned to face me, a mocking smile touching his lips. "A tender farewell, my lady. Have you no kiss for your loving husband?"

Color flooded my face. I drew near and kissed him, dutifully. He gave a short, hard laugh.

"Try not to miss me too much."

With an introduction by the Moultons I found I had an easy entree into the social life of the British colony. It appeared that the wife of an American clipper captain was considered an interesting *parti*, and I had no lack of invitations to garden parties and teas, formal dinners and government functions. One could almost, I reflected, forget one was in Hong Kong were it not for the uncomfortable equatorial sun.

But Edna Moulton was determined that I should see the other side of China, too. We made numerous expeditions by sedan chair and rickshaw to Hindu temples, graceful tea pagodas, and the stunning homes of wealthy Chinese merchants. In cruel contrast were the glimpses of unbelievable poverty. I learned that thousands of coolies lived with only the clothes on their backs and a bundle of possessions tied to the end of a stick. Other families were jammed into tiny bamboo huts or tattered sampans. Crippled, skeleton-thin beggars confronted us at every turn. Edna told me that some deliberately maimed themselves to attract a sympathetic handout.

But it was the open markets that most fascinated me. We spent whole afternoons examining the lovely silks, or watching craftsmen create works of beauty, carvings of wood and ivory, at their benches. I was delighted by the open-air theater performances; horrified by hawkers who offered snakes for dinner. At one stall we saw young girls being sold as casually as loaves of bread.

Perhaps it was not so surprising that with all these new and exciting experiences I sometimes forgot to be homesick. What did disconcert me, however, was the discovery that I missed Joshua.

On the occasions that we visited Frederick Moulton's offices on the waterfront, I found my gaze wandering to the *Neptune's Car.* The clipper looked deserted, somehow vulnerable. I wondered, with all the talk about pirates, if she was really safe.

"Joshua paid protection money before he left," the Moultons assured me. "The pirates will leave the ship alone."

"What about the monsoons?" I persisted. I'd heard that the last storm dragged several anchored vessels onto the rocks. I know Joshua would consider himself responsible if anything happened to the *Neptune's Car* in his absence. The Moultons were sympathetic but not concerned.

"I rather think your worry is for Joshua, my dear," said Edna. "That's only natural. But do try not to believe the worst."

"Why should I be worried? Joshua is perfectly capable of taking care of himself."

"Of course he is. Joshua knows his way around these parts better than any man I know."

"I assure you I haven't the least doubt of that, Mrs. Moulton!" I cried, exasperated.

She took out a handkerchief and dabbed at her eyes. "Such a brave child. I must confess that after three weeks without a word from him. . . . But you're right not to let these rumors disturb you."

"Rumors?"

"Now you've done it, Edna!" said her exasperated husband. "I told you she probably hadn't seen anything in the papers."

I fought off a sudden feeling of dread. "Mr. Moulton? What are you talking about?"

"Nothing at all, dear girl, I do assure you. Only a small item in the newspaper about a white man that was found floating in the Pearl River. A sailor. No doubt he was the victim of a Hog Lane grog shop or a flower boat—"

"Floating brothels, that's what they are!" contributed Edna. "Any man that sets foot on one of those is asking for trouble."

"Was there no—identification of the body?"

Mr. Moulton sighed. "The man was fair, medium height and frame. That's all they could say."

"Then it could be Joshua, couldn't it? He was on the Pearl River, going to Canton."

"It could be any one of hundreds of men by that description. We must be rational about this."

"So right, Frederick. This sort of thing happens all the time in China. If it's not thieves or pirates murdering people off, it's the fever."

"I don't think you are being much comfort, Edna."

"Dear me." She looked contrite. "I was only trying to look at the bright side."

As the weeks passed into a month I began to notice the Moultons' friends casting furtive glances of sympathy in my direction. It made me uncomfortable, although I was certain nothing could have happened to Joshua. I attended fewer social functions and spent the evenings writing long letters home, compulsively eating sweets.

A ship arrived with letters from Boston. I tore into the first and read the news of my brother George's marriage.

"How could he get married without me!" I cried, bursting into tears. "It isn't fair! He should have waited."

"I'm sure you don't really mean that, dear," admonished Edna Moulton. "You wouldn't deny your brother one moment of the happiness you and Joshua enjoy?"

I cried even harder. She urged me to open the other letters, and I found one from Andrew, which cheered me considerably.

"He says he's sailing for China! That was weeks ago, so he might arrive here any time! He writes, 'Wouldn't it be lucky if our paths should cross? If they do we must celebrate, that is, if a captain's wife is not too high and mighty for the company of a lowly second mate.' Oh, wouldn't it be lovely, Edna!"

"A reunion." She was at once enthusiastic. "We must have a dinner party."

"You'll like Drew. He's terribly good looking, and fun to be with. He even makes Joshua laugh."

"Your brother sounds a lot like you."

"I'm afraid I haven't made Joshua laugh for a very long time, Edna."

"He loves you. That's plain to see."

Was it? I sighed. Perhaps Joshua had loved me, before this nightmarish voyage. Now, whatever feeling had once been between us seemed to be trampled, crushed beyond recognition. I doubted if love would ever again be possible.

Edna misinterpreted my gloomy expression. "He'll be all right, my dear," she said softly. "We must keep up our spirits."

After another two weeks passed in silence, however, even the Moultons' spirits wavered. They held low-voiced conferences at meal-times as I ate through each course in stalwart silence.

"Do you think, Frederick, you ought to make inquiries?"

"Already taken care of, my love. A fortnight ago. Sent instructions to all my agents up the coast."

I said, with my mouth full, "Hadn't we better notify the *Neptune's* owners about Joshua's absence?"

"Dear girl, it is far too early to be taking such drastic measures."

"It's been six weeks. We have to face facts," I swallowed. From somewhere in another part of the house came a commotion of voices. I went on, "You have both been most kind, but I cannot take unfair advantage of your hospitality. If Joshua was not the man they found in the river we would have heard from him by now. The only thing for me to do is return home to Boston."

"I think not, my dear. Not just yet."

My fork clattered onto the plate. Edna Moulton jumped up and shrieked, "Joshua Patten! You horrid boy—walking in without a warning and giving us all a shock. Look at poor Mary. She's nearly overcome!"

His eyes fell on me cynically. "So I see."

"Where have you been, man?" demanded Frederick. "Had us thinking you were dead when that body turned up in the Pearl."

"I'm afraid I didn't know anything about that. When nothing came of my visit to Canton I went to Amoy and then followed a lead to Foochow. It paid off."

"You might have sent word."

"I did, as a matter of fact. Unfortunately, messages sometimes go astray."

I was uncomfortably aware that his eyes had not moved away from me.

"Well, sit down, sit down, my boy, and tell us all about it!"

"*Frederick.*"

He looked around. "What is it now, Edna?"

"Don't you think we ought to give the captain and Mary a little time alone together?"

"Well, I don't know if that's really—" Joshua began.

Mrs. Moulton hushed her husband and herded him from the room, then returned to enfold us both in an emotional embrace.

"God bless you, my dears."

The door closed. I said, feeling embarrassed, "So. Here we are again!"

"Yes."

He didn't move.

"I worried about you, Joshua. I really did."

He said nothing, but as his eyes moved over me I flushed self-consciously. I was still gaining weight.

"I'm not the sort to pine away to skin and bones. You know that."

"I am glad to find you well. Were the Moultons kind to you? Did they introduce you to their friends?"

"Oh, yes! Edna and I had wonderful times. And there were no end of invitations, more than I could accept, until—well, until people started wondering if something had happened to you."

"I'm sorry if that dampened your social life," he said dryly.

"What a terrible thing to say! Naturally, we were all concerned." I moved over to him and put my arms around his neck. "I got a letter from Drew, Joshua. He said he expects to come to Hong Kong. Isn't that exciting?"

"Of course. I'm always glad to see Andrew." He removed my hands and stepped back. "I have to go to the ship now. There are some matters to discuss with Buckley."

"But you're so tired! Surely that can wait until tomorrow. The Moultons will be disappointed—"

"I'll sleep better aboard the *Neptune's Car*."

The words were like a slap in the face. *So*, I thought, *he still hasn't forgiven me*. Had I expected him to? Did it matter?

"Very well. I suppose we'll be sailing soon to Foochow?"

"In a week or two. The tea won't be ready until the end of this month."

The Moultons, when they heard the news, made a great fuss until Joshua agreed that we would stay with them until our departure. It was for my sake, I knew. He would have preferred very much to return to the *Neptune's Car*.

There was a constraint between us that I did not know how to dissolve. A few times he asked if I wanted to take a carriage ride through the city or a stroll through the green hills. I went eagerly, but we ended up speaking very little. His indifference was even more frightening than hostility.

Often our walks took us near the waterfront. The harbor was always a scene of hectic activity, with ships loading or off-loading from all parts of the world. My hope of seeing Andrew before we left ebbed each day, and I thought wistfully, *If only he had come. It might have made a difference.*

On one such occasion that we paused to make conversation with another captain and his wife, newly arrived in Hong Kong. Joshua's eyes, as usual, strayed in the direction of his ship. Suddenly he froze.

Something was very wrong aboard the *Neptune's Car*. Even across the water we could hear the angry shouts, the excited gestures of the mates. And then, as we watched, several of the crew members darted to the fife rail and drew out the iron belaying pins.

"Stay where you are," he yelled at me. Jumping into a nearby tanka boat, he ordered the owner to row him to the ship.

"Joshua, wait." I ran to the edge of the quay but he didn't hear me. The small boat pulled steadily closer to the hull of the *Neptune's Car*. In another moment, he would be upon her.

"You've got to help him, captain." I clutched the sleeve of the big man next to me. He blinked.

"What can I do?"

"Yes, what can he do?" squeaked his wife, clutching his other arm for all she was worth.

"Joshua can't take on all those men by himself. He'll be killed!"

"Unless I'm off my reckoning," drawled the captain, "that crew is in more danger than your husband, ma'am."

The tanka boat was now bobbing alongside the clipper. Joshua sprang onto the rope ladder and scaled it with the swiftness of a cat. My heart pounded. At any moment the men would discover him, turn on him. But it seemed they were too involved with the officers.

Finally he stood outlined against the sky. I saw him extend his arm, saw the sun glinting on the metallic object he held in his hand.

The captain's wife saw it the same time I did, and screamed, "A gun! I can't look!"

Aboard the *Neptune's Car* the sailors all at once became aware of Joshua's presence. A deathly silence fell, and for a moment they stood as if paralyzed. Then, to a man, they turned and streaked toward the bow. Joshua followed them.

"That's it, Patten!" roared the captain. "After those scoundrels and teach 'em a lesson!"

"Henry! You don't think he'll murder them, do you?"

The crew was apparently wondering the same thing. They crawled on the bowsprit and out onto the jibboom as far as they could; then they began dropping into the bay.

The captain chuckled. "Scared witless. That water's full of sharks."

His wife whimpered. I felt an overwhelming urge to clobber them both. Fortunately a nearby British ship, the *Retribution,* took in the situation and, having a manned cutter available, dispatched it to pick up the men.

A few days later the Moultons held their farewell dinner party for us. By then everyone in Hong Kong knew about the mutiny, and Joshua was pressed for details. He was uncommunicative, however. He would only say that the troublemakers had been handed over to the American Consul.

"I'll wager you had no trouble signing on another crew," one guest observed. "We've a harbor chock full of vessels without cargos and sailors out of work."

"Too bad about the *Westward Ho,* eh?" Frederick Moulton winked at us as he told the others, "Captain Hussey couldn't secure a charter for England so he agreed to transport coolie slaves to the Callao guano deposits. Poor devil—he'll never get the stink out of his hold."

Joshua's jaw clenched as though he were struggling to control his temper. "I don't suppose we should spare any pity for the 'poor devils' he's transporting?"

"What's that? I'm afraid I don't catch your meaning, Patten."

"It's not really hard to understand. Those Chinese slaves will die in those pits, either from exhaustion or disease. Most of them don't survive beyond a few months. That's murder, isn't it?"

The company all looked as though they had bones caught in their throats. Mrs. Moulton made an effort to lighten the situation.

"My dear, the coolie trade isn't so very different from the African slave trade. Most of the blacks on your American plantations manage to survive, do they not?"

"Many who survive wish they hadn't, I'm afraid. I would find it difficult to recommend one form of slavery over another."

I began an enthusiastic account of the abolition movement and Mrs. Stowe's *Uncle Tom's Cabin.* No one seemed inclined to join in, however, and after a while the subject was dropped. The next day Joshua and I made our farewells and boarded the *Neptune's Car.*

It was an odd feeling, re-entering our quarters after so long. I had expected to face the moment with grim resignation and so was taken by surprise by the comfortable familiarity that assailed me. It was almost as if I was coming home.

Joshua was watching me curiously. "Not exactly the luxurious accommodations you've become used to, these two months."

"No. I enjoyed my stay with the Moultons."

"Well, cheer up, my love. You won't have to put up with this crude life much longer."

"I didn't mean—"

"I know what you meant. And you'll be happy to know I've made up my mind. Once we get back to Boston I will never ask you to leave it again as long as you live."

It was what I had wanted to hear all these months. Why didn't I feel elated?

"You see, having a child was never as important to me as you seemed to think. I would like a son some day, but I was hoping for something else between us on this voyage, what you might call a marriage of minds. It probably never had a chance. The irony is you don't even know what I'm talking about."

He left me. As his boots rung hollowly on the companion-way steps I felt a sudden, compelling need to call out, to go after him and tell him that perhaps I did, after all, understand.

Then the moment passed. And it was too late.

chapter
12

On September 29th, the *Neptune's Car* weighed anchor and left the protected harbor of Hong Kong, steering for the Formosa Strait. Every member of the crew carried a firearm. Tension lined every face. The number of ships that had disappeared after a pirate attack in these waters did not bear thinking about.

Under other circumstances I might have enjoyed the passage. The sea was calm, the breeze warm and pleasant. The clipper flew like a bird released from its cage.

"She's glad to be movin' again," said the mate, unusually talkative. "Just wish we were pointin' south instead of north. Won't breathe easy till this whole Chiny coast is under our stern."

"At least there's been no sign of pirates."

"Beggin' your pardon, ma'am, it ain't the pirates makin' me nervous so much as the thought o' that river ahead."

"River?"

"Only way to get to Foochow from the sea. It's called the Min. Twenty-five of the narrowest, crookedest miles in

China. And a mean current to boot. You wanta know what turned my hair grey? It was the Min, last time through."

I paled.

"But don't you worry, ma'am. If'n the cap'n could handle a tight spot like Le Maire he can handle the Min."

"Even though he's never navigated it before?"

He shrugged. "Has to be a first time for everythin', don't there, ma'am?"

At the mouth of the river we took on a pilot. I debated whether to seal myself into the cabin or face my fate on deck. I opted for the latter, simply because I couldn't bear not knowing what was going on. Our progress was painfully slow. We dared use only a fraction of sail since there was no room to maneuver. To our right and left rocks flanked us like jagged teeth. Showing pale through the green waters were the treacherous sand bars. When I sent the steward for cool drinks Joshua drank his absently, never relaxing his attention from the wind and current.

The passage took only a few hours, but it seemed like days before we emerged, free and clear, into the beautiful Pagoda Anchorage. The sight of it drew from me an involuntary exclamation of delight. The harbor was cloverleaf-shaped, set like a blue jewel amidst the emerald mountains.

"Look at all the temples dotting the hills, Joshua! Do you think we might visit some of them?"

"If you like. There should be time while they're doing the loading."

"But I want to see that, too. Mr. Buckley told me all about it."

"Did he, now? Since when did you two start talking to each other?"

"I think he must have missed me these two months! He's been almost nice since I came aboard."

"Perhaps he missed your cooking," Joshua suggested. "Let's hope the peace and harmony continues."

The process of stowing tea in the hold of a ship was, I learned, almost an art, accomplished with swift precision. First came ballast—large quantities of scrap metal and stones—to offset the lightness of the cargo. Then came the tea, the most inferior grade first, in case the ship leaked. Each chest was wedged in tightly and nailed down to utilize every square inch and to keep the cargo from shifting. As a final protection against dampness, the chests were covered with layers of split bamboo and canvas.

Our stay in Foochow was brief. Just before we were to make the tortuous journey out to the sea again Joshua took me to see the temples. There he announced very casually that he had decided the *Neptune's Car* would take on passengers.

"Passengers!" I was incredulous. "You said you'd never carry any. You told me they were a nuisance!"

"I was prevailed upon this time to make an exception. Mrs. Jordan-Chadwick was recently widowed in a malaria epidemic. She finds it expedient for her and her two children to return to their family estate in England. And she is prepared to pay handsomely for the privilege."

"There must be other ships that could accommodate her."

"Really, Mary," he said with exasperation. "I expected you to be pleased. You're always harping you have no other women to talk to."

"She has two children, you say?"

"A boy and a girl, five and seven. There's an *amah* to take care of them."

"Well, I hope she's the agreeable sort."

"I found her most agreeable," he said. That should have warned me.

An hour before sailing, as Joshua stood frowning at the

timepiece in his hand, a carriage clattered onto the quay and disgorged two plump, cherubic-looking children; an elderly Chinese woman, who was evidently the nursemaid; and the elegantly attired Mrs. Louise Jordan-Chadwick. I disliked her on sight.

Calling for her children to hurry, she moved gracefully up the gangplank. As she came closer I took in the tumble of golden curls underneath the grey bonnet, the flawless alabaster complexion. When she stepped onto the deck she stood at least six inches taller than I, which put her large, delphinium eyes on exactly the same level as Joshua's. The fact did not escape either of us.

"Captain Patten, I do hope we have not delayed you?"

The captain stared, transfixed, until my elbow dug into his ribs.

"Delayed? Not at all. Allow me to introduce Mrs. Patten. Mary—Mrs. Jordan-Chadwick."

"But you didn't tell me what a child she is, captain! Do call me Louise, my dear. And these are my angels, Eustacia and Gerald. Stop punching your sister, Gerald. What a pity you and the captain have no children of your own."

She looked from one to the other of us. My smile petrified.

"My darlings have been such a comfort during my bereavement. You cannot imagine, Mary dear, how dreadful it is to be without a husband! How entirely helpless one feels."

"You are quite right, Louise dear. I cannot imagine."

Joshua shot me a warning glance. "Perhaps you would care to see your staterooms now, madam. The steward will conduct you. I hope you will find them adequate. The children are to share their quarters with the nurse."

"Cheng-Li will see that they give you no trouble, captain."

"Excellent. When you are settled perhaps you'll join us on the quarterdeck."

Try to keep her away, I thought. The slim grey back moved off.

"Joshua, how long did you say it would take us to reach England?"

"Four months, give or take a few weeks."

I sighed. I had the uncomfortable certainty I was going to hate every moment of it. I was right, of course.

Down the Min River and South China Sea, across the Indian Ocean and around the Cape of Good Hope, all the way to the dominion of Great Britain I ate, slept, and drank the heavenly Louise. She spent very little time in her quarters, preferring to arrange herself artistically in a deck chair with a book. Nor did she once miss a meal at the captain's table. In vain did I wait for the paragon to become seasick.

Cheng-Li, on the other hand, was unable to lift her head from the moment the anchor was aweigh until it rattled down fifteen thousand miles later. The "angels," after surviving the briefest bout of sickness, tore around the ship harassing the crew until Joshua sternly ordered me to keep them amused.

"*Me?*" I squeaked with indignation. "I have my hands full caring for Cheng-Li. Why can't their mother bestir herself?"

"Louise is not strong. She has been through a lot."

"Strong enough to twist you around her finger."

He regarded me with an arched brow. "If I didn't know you so well, I could almost believe you were jealous."

"I simply resent being a laughingstock. It must be obvious to everyone on this ship you spend more time with the merry widow than with me."

His voice hardened. "I thought that was the way you preferred it."

"You don't usually concern yourself with what I prefer."

"Louise is our guest," he said abruptly. "I will continue to treat her with courtesy, and you will do the same."

The temperature between us dropped in contrast to the weather on deck. Christmas approached as we sailed just off the coast of Africa, but I could summon little enthusiasm. In an effort to keep the children occupied we baked sugar cookies for the crew and contrived decorations for the saloon.

The morning of December 25th dawned hot and clear. I dressed in a summer-weight green shirtwaist for the service to be held amidships, trying not to think of other, happier Christmases back home.

Louise arrived on deck twenty minutes after everyone else. She was elaborately coiffed and gowned in cool white organdy and looked like the angel on top of a tree. The men fixed their gaze on her with something akin to adoration. Then, to my disgust, she was prevailed upon (without much coaxing), to sing an English carol.

"Now," she said sweetly, when she had finished, "we must have a song from our dear Mary!"

I shook my head. "I couldn't."

"Surely you can. You are too modest."

"I told you, I can't sing!" I felt hot and awkward and absurdly close to tears. Joshua frowned.

"Perhaps Eustacia and Gerald will favor us with a carol or two."

They complied promptly, quavering off-key. Joshua followed this up with the reading of the Christmas story.

Somehow it all seemed so meaningless and out of place. Christmas was cold weather and blazing fires, the bustle of a big city and cozy gatherings of friends. Robbed of all tradition, the day was like any other. The story of a baby's birth hundreds of years ago held little significance.

Eustacia and Gerald, at least, did not appear to mind the

strangeness of celebrating the holiday while suspended between continents. The whole voyage was doubtless an adventure to them. After the service the crew presented the children with sleds they had painstakingly fashioned. I thought this extremely good-hearted considering the trouble the men had endured from them. Louise had brought with her a whole chestful of toys for the occasion. For me there were a half dozen lace handkerchiefs, and for Joshua, an elegant pair of gold cuff links.

I was dismayed. I, too, had purchased cuff links for Joshua! But they were obviously of lesser value. How could I possibly give them to him now?

I fretted all through the elaborately contrived dinner of chicken, tinned cranberries, plum pudding and pie. Then I shut myself in the cabin, wallowing in self-pity. The heat was stifling, but at least I would not have to encounter the detestable Louise. I passed the time devising ways to get rid of her.

There were footsteps on the companionway. I grabbed a book.

"What in the world are you doing down here?" Joshua demanded. "It's suffocating."

"It's also the only place on this ship one can have any privacy."

"You'd do better reading if the book were right side up."

I burst into tears, and he sighed.

"Mary, Mary, what is it now?"

"That wretched Louise. I hate her! She spoils everything. Why did she have to give you cuff links? I—I was going to give you cuff links."

"Well? There's no tragedy in that. I can use two pairs."

"But hers are much nicer!" Hiccuping, I went to the drawer in the next room and brought them back. "You see? These are only ebony and silver. It was all I could afford."

He considered them. "Would you believe me if I said I liked this pair better?"

I shook my head.

"Perhaps this will cheer you up." From inside his jacket he withdrew a narrow velveted case and opened the clasp. Inside lay a delicate jade necklace, exquisitely fashioned.

"Oh, Joshua. It's beautiful!"

He fastened it around my throat and smiled. "And so are you, my lady. Look in the glass."

"It does rather flatter me, doesn't it? Joshua, do you think I'm as beautiful as Louise?"

He groaned. "Why must every conversation on this voyage revolve around that woman?"

"I just wish I knew what you find so fascinating about her."

"She is pleasant, witty, intelligent. Commodities which are in short supply these days."

"Where are you going?"

"On deck, where there's a breeze."

"I'll come with you."

"Not unless you are prepared to associate amiably with our passengers."

He walked out. I stared after him in fury and then hurled the book at the door.

"I *knew* you liked her cuff links better!"

The weeks following Christmas I kept a vigilant watch on quarterdeck activities until a chill forced me below. Louise displayed a singular hardiness for one so purportedly frail, and it seemed to me I saw even less of Joshua than usual. He had, he said, undertaken supervision of the children. They missed their father. I seethed in silence, trying to ignore the gnawing edge of worry.

Finally the day came when the *Neptune's Car* sailed past the Bay of Biscay and we entered the English Channel. Nothing could keep me from the rail as we sighted land; I was as excited as the children when we paused at Dungeness Light for the pilot. Then it was through the Strait of Dover to the mouth of the Thames, where the sails were furled and a steam tug pulled us up-river to London Wharf.

London! All my life I had listened to tales about this city from Mama and Papa. Now I would see it for myself— Queen Victoria's residence at Windsor, the Houses of Parliament, the Tower. I hoped there would be time for everything.

Confusion broke loose as the *Neptune's Car* was moored by the quayside. Mr. Buckley bawled orders to the crew, threatening no pay until the gear was neatly stowed or coiled. Gerald and Eustacia ran screaming from bow to stern getting in everybody's way. Cheng-Li, upon being notified that we had reached our destination, rallied sufficiently to stagger down the gangplank.

"I do hope you will be able to manage, Louise," I said sweetly as we waited for Joshua to corral the children. For once their mother looked harassed. "You did say you are traveling to your family's estate in the north of England?"

"Eventually, yes. But we will stay for a short while with my late husband's family in London. There is some business to attend."

"Oh." This was unwelcome news. "Joshua didn't mention that."

"Didn't he?" She smiled as he came up with her children in tow. "It must have slipped his mind. How naughty of you Joshua, to forget my invitation!"

He looked blank.

"You remember, I asked you to meet my husband's

brother, the one who has a controlling interest in one of the tea companies. I am sure he will be prepared to offer you a very fair price for your cargo."

Joshua's face cleared. "I would be honored to meet him, Mrs. Jordan-Chadwick."

"Such formality, captain! You must call me Louise, now that we're old friends."

Her eyes locked with his until I blew loudly into my handkerchief.

"Poor Mary. Such a frightful cold! Do take care our English climate doesn't make it worse."

"I shall be most careful, Louise, dear."

"Excellent! Goodbye, then. It's been a pleasure."

Joshua jabbed me in the ribs. I took her proffered hand.

"Forgive my angels for not coming close for a hug. Nasty germs, you know! Eustacia, sweet, stop kicking your brother."

We watched them go down the gangplank. I sighed. "Isn't it wonderful to be in England? Let's celebrate!"

"Where would you like to go?"

I tried fluttering my lashes like Louise. "Who said we have to go anywhere?"

"Are you serious? After four months cooped up on this clipper? I thought you'd be the first down the gangplank."

We settled into a quaint hotel in Chelsea, and dined that evening on steak and kidney pie in the hotel's ancient dining room. After the first night in a huge canopied bed, I woke stretching contentedly.

"How glorious to sleep in a bed that doesn't rock."

Joshua, already up and dressed, shrugged. "Seems unnatural to me." He drew the curtains. "Raining. Too bad. You'll have to postpone your sightseeing."

"You're going out."

"Of course. I have business."

"You intend to see that Louise creature again, don't you?"

"I am going to her brother-in-law's offices."

"Ha! She'll be lurking about somewhere, you can count on it." I brooded as he brushed his best coat. "Why don't you let me go with you?"

"You know why. It's wet and miserable, you'd only make your cold worse, and you'd be bored out of your mind."

"I'll be bored sitting in this hotel!"

"Patience." He bent and kissed me hurriedly. "Maybe we can go somewhere special tonight."

I loafed in bed all morning, drinking tea and reading the newspapers. The advertisements were most engrossing. I studied the latest fashions in bonnets and gowns, wishing aggrievedly that I could visit the shops in person. But why shouldn't I? It was unreasonable of Joshua to expect me to hang about here, cold or no cold.

I rose determinedly and dressed. Leaving a note for Joshua on the unlikely chance that he returned before I did, I departed for Harrods.

The outing was immensely successful. The variety and quality of everything made it necessary to lavish delightful hours in making comparisons, but it also made me later than expected getting back to the hotel. The desk clerk confirmed my fear that Joshua had preceded me.

He'll be furious, I thought, opening the door.

I found him sitting in an ornate chair by the window, holding a letter. He rose when I came in.

"So you're back."

"Don't be angry, Joshua. I just couldn't stay in this room another minute." I sneezed.

"You've taken more cold."

"No. I just—" I sneezed again, and he crossed to pull the bell rope. "I'll order hot water."

He spoke absently, as though he were distracted by something. I was relieved. "I had the most marvelous time, Joshua! You should see how much the styles have changed. I feel positively dowdy. Did we get mail from home? That looks like Papa's handwriting."

"Yes. I'll tell you about it after you've had your bath."

The hot water felt delicious. I soaked until it was cold, then rubbed myself briskly and slipped into a robe. Joshua still stood by the window, staring out at the rain.

"How did your business go? Did you get a good price for the tea?"

"The owners should be pleased enough."

"I'm glad. Now maybe you'll have time to show me around London!" I sat down at the dressing table to uncoil and brush my hair. "What did Papa have to say? It must be important. He hates to write."

"It's about your brother, Mary."

"Andrew? It must be," I laughed. "George never gets into mischief. What's he done now?"

Joshua came over to me and took the brush from my hand. He set it down.

"Mary. I don't know how to tell you this. Your father thought it would be better coming from me, maybe because I loved him, too, like a brother."

My mouth went dry. I stood up and turned around to face him.

"What do you mean?"

"Andrew is gone, Mary. . . . He's dead."

"No." I shook my head.

"His ship went down in a storm off Cornwall. All hands were lost."

"That can't be true. No! I won't believe it. Not Drew."

"My darling." His eyes held infinite pity. "Your father went to great lengths to be certain. I'm afraid there can be no doubt."

The terrible pain of what he was saying sliced through me. I crumpled, and Joshua held me tightly.

"Why Andrew?" I cried as a wild storm of weeping threatened to overwhelm me. "How could God let it happen to him? He was too young to die." I lifted tear-blurred eyes to Joshua and saw a reflection of my own agony.

"I don't have the answers, Mary. I wish I did. I loved him, too."

Andrew had been easy to love—warm, laughing, eager for everything life could offer him, and eager to give in return. I thought of the water closing over his head, and whispered,

"He must have been so afraid!"

"For an instant, perhaps. But I don't think your brother was afraid of what lay beyond that storm. We talked about it once. Men at sea face death more than most men do."

"If only I could have seen him, just once more. I never really told him what he meant to me."

"He knew." Joshua spoke softly. "He always said he didn't know how you could fight like cat and dog with somebody and love them so much. Drew was always telling me about you. I think he had it planned, from the day we met, that we would marry. Practically dragged me to Boston that first time. You were still a child when I married you. I was afraid I would lose you if I waited. But it was too soon. Your feeling for me was too fragile. It didn't survive."

"Joshua—"

"Let me finish. I thought if you came on this voyage you might learn to love the sea as I do. It was a mistake. It's a harsh and lonely way of life for a woman. It turned whatever love you had left for me into hatred."

"My dear."

I drew a deep, shuddering breath and hid my face against his chest. "I thought it was you who hated me!"

"You should know better than that."

"But after that time in China, when I deceived you, you were so distant and cold!"

"Giving you sea room to decide what you really wanted."

"Waiting for me to grow up? Oh, my love, why did it take so long?"

He framed my face with his hands and gazed urgently down. "Andrew knew us better than we knew ourselves. We've wasted so much time. . . . Thank God it's not too late!"

Joshua's lips met mine, first with gentleness and then, as I responded, with mounting passion. He carried me to the massive oak bed. And there, still in each other's arms, the darkness passed into dawn.

Chapter
13

Our business in London was quickly discharged. Joshua
had small difficulty securing a charter for New York, and
during the loading he took me to view some of the famous
monuments of the city.

But somehow, my eagerness to see them had vanished. I
knew what a blow Andrew's death would be to my family, to
my mother and father especially, and I wanted to be with
them.

Joshua understood this. His strength was the only firm
thing for me to cling to in the quicksand of my emotions.
Each day it seemed I fell more and more in love with him.

I was ready when it came time to board the *Neptune's Car*.
The ship was our home now, and the isolation imposed on us
at sea was no longer a thing to be feared. After all we had
been through, I was sure, the short crossing to New York
could present no new problems. But there I was wrong.

February and March are not prime months for sailing in
the North Atlantic. Icy westerlies hurled themselves against
us unceasingly along with a whole catalog of other nasty

weather conditions—rain, snow, sleet, and hail, plus one or two severe thunderstorms thrown in for good measure.

Our clipper was no longer the dancing thoroughbred she had once been. Her keel was fouled and crusted with barnacles, and our progress was labored.

Thunderstorms at sea always made me particularly nervous. There is something about being the only standing object in an area hundreds of miles wide that betrays your vulnerability. When I stood at the rail beside Joshua watching the giant white jagged fingers rake the sky above, I could not repress a shiver. If one of those deadly fingers chanced to brush our masts . . .

Joshua made light of my fears. He reminded me of the lightning lines dropped overboard as a safety precaution.

"But we could still be struck by lightning," I persisted.

"There is always the possibility."

"And what would happen if we were set afire, with no one about to come to our rescue?"

He sighed. "If the rain or the crew failed to put out the fire, naturally, the ship would be lost."

"And so would everybody aboard."

"Yes. But it's highly unlikely, Mary. Stop worrying, will you?"

It started to rain after that conversation, so I went below and read awhile before going to bed. The storm was growing worse. I got into bed and pulled a blanket over my head to muffle the sound. Eventually, I dropped off.

All at once a crack like cannonfire exploded into the cabin. The *Neptune's Car* quivered from bow to stern. I sat bolt upright. We had been struck—there wasn't a doubt in my mind.

"Joshua!" I screamed. I threw off the bedclothes and groped feverishly in the dark for something to put on. Above there were shouts and sounds of running. Were we afire, then? In my mind's eye I saw crew members battling smoke and flames and my stomach lurched. Where was Joshua? I had to find him.

I opened the cabin door and stumbled up the steps, into the night. It was raining—hard. There was no fire, then. But why all the—?

At that moment, I saw the men clustered in a circle of light by the deckhouse. They were bending over the crumpled forms of two men. My heart stopped beating.

"*Joshua!*"

Instantly one of the kneeling forms rose and came toward me. It was my beloved husband. I wrapped my arms around him, heedless of the watching men.

"Thank God you're all right!"

"What about you?" he asked.

"Just frightened. What happened?"

"A bolt struck the foremast. Sorenson and Krueger were thrown from the rigging and one of them hit the deckhouse."

"What can I do?"

He hesitated. "It isn't pretty, Mary."

"Please."

"All right. I'll get them below. You fetch the medicine chest, blankets, and whatever you can find for bandages. We'll have to make splints."

It was well that Joshua warned me. The sight of crushed bones and blood made me want to turn and run. Not even Sinbad's injuries had been as bad. But then I became too busy to think of myself. We worked over the men the rest of the night.

By some miracle, they were still alive several days later when we sighted Sandy Hook. As I finished my packing I could hear the men on deck singing, and I found myself humming along with them.

I thought I heard the skipper say,
    Leave her, Johnnie, leave her!
Tomorrow you will get your pay—
    It's time for us to leave her.

The work was hard, the voyage was long,
    Leave her, Johnnie, leave her!
The seas were high, the gales were strong,
    It's time for us to leave her.

When I was through I sat down with my journal. There was time for one last entry:

I have been around the world, and have seen things I never dreamed of seeing. I have felt the blistering cruelty of the sun at the equator and the bone-numbing cold of Cape Horn; I have known the terror of a typhoon, and the marvel of star-hung tropical nights. I have seen a California gambler and a Chinese mandarin and an English queen. I have experienced life and death and loneliness and fulfillment.

And I have fallen in love with the man who is my husband.

chapter
14

When Joshua handed over the ship's manifest in New York the owners ordered the *Neptune's Car* into drydock for a major overhaul. I was overjoyed. We would be free for almost four months.

Later I was to look upon that spring and early summer of the year 1856 as one of the most bittersweet periods of my life.

Boston had changed. A thousand small differences caught our attention as our carriage rolled over the cobbled streets. New buildings were under construction, and more vehicles and pedestrians than ever congested the thoroughfares. But if the city had altered, I was even more taken aback by changes in the people I had known. In the space of a single year, close acquaintances had wed or had children, suffered illness or tragedy or moved away.

Within the brick walls of my home on Salutation Street there was a stillness that had not been there before. With Andrew's death, my parents had changed radically. Much of Mama's spirit was missing. She said in a worried aside that Papa had had a bad spell with his heart. And he was unusually quiet—except when I described my visit to London.

"Did you see Queen Victoria?" Mama wanted to know.

"We caught a glimpse when she passed in her carriage. She looked every bit as regal as I expected her to be, in spite of her size."

"She was only a young thing when we left England," my father mused. And gradually he launched into stories about the England of his boyhood. The mood lightened.

Later, we went to see George and his bride in their home on Unity Street. Elsa was a tall, fresh-faced girl of German extraction, intelligent and cheerful.

"She will be good for you, George. You always took yourself too seriously."

"We can't all be adventurers like you and Andrew." He caught himself, and added. "He got to meet Elsa, you know. I'm glad of that."

Victoria and Robert's newest addition to their family was four weeks old when I saw her. My sister laid the warm little body in my arms and I gazed at her with awe.

"She looks too perfect to be real! You and Robert must be so happy."

"Oh, yes. Though I won't say that raising four little ones is without its challenges!"

Robert gave Joshua a friendly nudge. "Isn't it about time you and Mary started a family?"

We looked at each other. I said softly, "I think we'd both like that. Perhaps, after one more voyage together."

Much of our time we spent in Maine. Our first trip there had been too hasty for me to become well-acquainted with the place or the people. This time I wanted to walk through the village in which Joshua had grown up, linger in the store and schoolhouse and the church he had attended. I wanted to climb the hills surrounding the Patten homestead where he had gazed so many hours out to sea, dreaming. Perhaps then I would be able to understand those hidden spaces within him I had yet to touch.

One hill in particular became our favorite. Although we went on many outings around the countryside and along the coast, it was on this rise, overlooking the broad sweep of Penobscot Bay, that we spent our most pleasurable hours talking.

"I do like Maine, Joshua!" I exclaimed as we picnicked there one Sunday afternoon. "I like your family, too. Your mother and father—and even your sisters and their families have made me feel so welcome. They're like you. No matter how busy they get they have some quiet island they can go to inside that keeps them strong, and unworried." I laughed, only half joking. "You must tell me your secret."

He smiled and reached over to tug lazily at the ribbons of my bonnet. It tumbled off. "You never worry, do you, Mistress Mary?"

"All the time. I'm scared every minute I'm on your clipper. And I'd be even *more* scared if I weren't. Some hussy like that Jordan-Chadwick creature might get her clutches on you. Or—" I stopped.

"Or what?"

"Something worse might happen. Like what happened to Andrew. Aren't *you* ever afraid, Joshua?"

"Of course I am."

"But it's under control?"

"Not under my control."

I threw my bonnet at him. "Stop teasing me."

"All right. Let me ask you a question," he said, seriously. "Who's in charge of a vessel?"

"The captain, naturally."

"But even the captain has to obey the owner's orders. The owner decides a ship's destination or purpose. The master works to carry out that purpose."

"So?"

"Every man has the command of his life. But who owns it? Who owns your life, Mary?"

I was startled. "I do."

He nodded. "Unless by a deliberate act of will you sign the ownership over to someone else."

"That sounds like a dangerous proposition!"

"You'd have to be very sure of that person. Surer of him than you are of yourself."

"You can't be that certain of anyone," I declared. "Except God, maybe. You aren't going to tell me that in some mystical, magical way you gave your life to him?"

"It didn't happen overnight." His shoulders lifted. "There wasn't much that was 'magical' about, it either. My life had run aground, so to speak. God didn't get much of a deal.

"I had a girl, once," he continued, his eyes on the ocean, "right here in Thomaston. It was long before I met you. We grew up together, and probably would have married. Then, while I was at sea, Celia died in an influenza epidemic. I used that for an excuse for casting myself adrift from everything I learned in that little white church down the hill."

I listened to the recitation in astonishment. He might have been talking about another person.

"Drinking, gambling, fighting—they're all part of a sailor's life, and I considered myself no better or worse than my mates. But I was ambitious. I wanted a quarterdeck of my own some day. A few years before the gold rush I got a berth as second mate. The first mate got drunk and picked a quarrel—and the captain took his side. I lost my temper.

Inside of a few minutes I also lost my rank and, I believed then, all chances for advancement. Things went downhill after that. Finally I scraped bottom."

I shook my head. "I can't believe you're telling me this."

"It's true—all of it, plus a lot of sordid details I'll spare you. You've noticed, haven't you, I'm a little touchy about allowing liquor on my ship? That's for my sake as much as the crew's."

"I still don't understand what happened to you."

"I'm not *myself* anymore. That's what I've been trying to explain. I made a deliberate, unemotional agreement allowing God the controlling ownership of my life. Not that the decision came easily. First I had to get to know him better, trust him. The trust came when I understood how much he loved me."

"How can anybody really know God? Joshua, be reasonable. What makes you think he even wants us to give our lives to him?"

"Because he communicated with us, through the written word and 'the word made flesh'—his son. It's funny, but I used to think of the Bible as a dried up old history book with nothing in it for us today. Now I know it for what it is—a love letter from the Creator to his Creation, a revelation of himself so that we could really know him."

"You make him sound like a flesh-and-blood person."

"He's as real to me as you are. He's proved his love a hundred different ways. You say there's a part of me you can't seem to get close to. He's that part, Mary. And we will never know a perfect unity until you know him, and love him, as I do."

All at once, I had had enough. "Just listen to us! It's far too beautiful a day for such heavy discussion. I know it's important, my dear captain, but let's not talk about it today."

I retrieved my bonnet and tied it securely under my chin. Springing to my feet, I nudged him with one toe. "Race you to the bottom of the hill?"

To my relief Joshua didn't bring up the subject again. Our stay in Maine passed swiftly and soon we were saying our farewells. On the last visit to "our" hill, Joshua's father unexpectedly asked to come along.

"You two sure did take a fancy to this spot, didn't you? Poor piece for farmin', but I have to admit it's got a pretty view. Good for settin' a house on, maybe."

"I was meaning to speak to you about that, sir." Joshua studied his father's face. "We can't afford to buy property yet, never mind think about building. But I'd like to ask you for an option on the land. Maybe someday—"

"No, 'fraid I can't do that, son. Already made arrangements to transfer the title."

There was a short, disappointed silence. "I see," replied Joshua.

"Ayuh. Property's signed over to you and Mary, son. It's yours to build whenever you decide. I thought it was only right you two should have a home of your own."

Adam Patten clapped his son's shoulder and then strode off. We stared after him, astonished.

"It's all ours!" I laughed, flinging my arms around Joshua's neck. "Can you think of a more perfect place to raise our children?"

"It's a little isolated. You're a city girl, remember."

"*Was* a city girl. Now I'm a captain's wife. I'm used to being isolated, remember. Besides, how could I be lonely with a houseful of children?"

"Houseful, hm?" He grinned, pulling closer. "Maybe we ought to get started on that project."

"Joshua Patten. First we build the house. *Then* the children."

In June the owners sent word that the *Neptune's Car* was out of drydock. Joshua and I traveled to New York.

It was hard parting from my family once more. So much had happened during my last absence, and I was acutely aware of my father's frail health. We were all so terribly vulnerable! But even that knowledge could not keep me from sailing with my husband now.

It seemed that I was fated to visit New York in only extremes of weather. The wealthy had already left the city *en masse* because of the extreme heat, but it was still crowded. While Joshua was busy with last minute details I devoted myself to outfitting our cabin with all the basic luxuries he insisted we didn't need.

The *Neptune's Car* had never looked better. Scraped, painted, varnished, there wasn't another ship in the harbor— in my prejudiced opinion—that could match her in elegance. I thought it highly disloyal of Mr. Buckley to have gone off on another clipper a few months earlier, lured by a paltry raise in pay and the promise of advancement. Things would be dull without my old sparring partner.

I met the new first mate as I was staggering aboard after a shopping expedition. A man appeared from nowhere to relieve me of boxes and assist me onto the deck. I was still gasping my thanks when I noticed the way he was staring at me, and felt an odd prickling at the back of my neck.

By most standards he would be called attractive. He was tall, over six feet; slim and hard-muscled. Thick black hair fringed a narrow face with dark eyes and an aquiline nose. Yet something in his smile was vaguely disturbing. Had I been a cat my fur would have been standing on end.

"Mrs. Patten, I presume?"

"Yes. You must be our first officer. The captain mentioned your name. Keefer, isn't it?"

"Mr. Keeler."

"Ah, yes. Well," I chattered nervously, "how fortunate that you were on hand. Perhaps you wouldn't mind carrying those boxes below for me. Is the captain aboard?"

"Aye. He's below."

Absurd to feel relieved. Did I imagine the mate was going to clout me over the head? I rushed into the cabin rather breathlessly.

"Hello, darling! I found the most wonderful bargains today."

Joshua glanced up from the papers he was studying. "Just leave those boxes where you are, Keeler."

"Aye, sir." The mate deposited my things and went out. Joshua leaned back, smiling.

"Well, my love? What do you think of him? Quite a change from Buckley, eh?"

"Quite."

"He comes with excellent references."

"Not all from the ladies, I trust."

"I know nothing about that," he replied stiffly. "He's supposed to be a first-class seaman. That's all that concerns me."

"It's not all that concerns me," I sniffed.

"Would you care to elaborate? Was Mr. Keeler impolite to you just now?"

"Oh, he was polite enough. Too polite."

Joshua sighed. "You didn't like Buckley because he was coarse and you don't like Keeler because he's too polite. Will I ever understand you?"

"Probably not." I took off my bonnet and began unwrapping my purchases. "I wonder what our steward will be like?"

"As a matter of fact, I think you'll be pleased. He's an old friend of yours. When I ran into him today the scoundrel had the nerve to request double the wages he got before."

"*Manolo!*" I cried. "You agreed, I hope?"

"I certainly did not. But he'll sign on. He knows an easy berth when he sees one."

The night before sailing the owners and their wives invited us to dine at Del Monicos. I was pleased to note that the men's attitude toward Joshua had been transformed dramatically from belligerence to respect. Their wives positively hung on his every word. Fortunately, nothing was required of me in the way of conversation. I was able to devote myself entirely to the enjoyment of my food.

When we got back to the ship we lingered in the sweet summer coolness on deck.

"What a marvelous night! My only regret is that I could eat so little of those fabulous pastries for dessert."

"You managed to astound the ladies, I think."

"Ha! *They* were more interested in devouring you. I had no idea clipper ship captains attracted so much adoration. I shall have to keep close to you."

"Mm. The closer the better."

"Joshua!"

"Just listen to how quiet it is. No one but you and me—"

"—and the officers."

"—and the *Neptune's Car*, tugging at her mooring, anxious to be off!"

"No more anxious than you, I'll warrant." I yawned. "You probably wish it was daylight already."

"No. There you are wrong, my lady. I wouldn't trade this night for all the sailings in the world."

And he proceeded, in the most gratifying way, to prove it.

part 3
THE SECOND VOYAGE

"My bounty is as boundless as the sea,
    My love as deep;
The more I give to thee, the more I have . . .
    For both are infinite."

—William Shakespeare

chapter
15

My hope that our second voyage to California would not turn into another race was a vain one. When I learned that we were sailing within twenty-four fours of *both* the *Intrepid* and *Romance of the Seas,* I groaned inwardly.

However, the first week passed with surprising sedateness. I allowed myself to believe this voyage would bear no resemblance to the one eighteen months before. Indeed, how could it? My captain was no more my keeper, nor was I any longer the little girl he had carried, against her will, from the life she held most dear.

Sometimes as I leaned against the rail under the July sun, watching Joshua scan the sails and then turn to rap out an order, I would wonder if this coolly competent individual even recalled that I was aboard. Then his gaze would fall on me, and I would see the blue-grey eyes kindle, and all my doubts would flee.

Not, of course, that it was all smooth sailing. Joshua still had his obstinate moments. When I suggested that I might more profitably spend my Sunday mornings sleeping late rather than attending worship services, one might have thought I was proposing treason.

"It is traditional for the captain's wife to attend," he insisted. "You should set a good example."

"Oh, Joshua, don't be so stuffy. Why should we both have to be good examples? Just one little morning."

I snuggled down into the bed and he dragged the covers off me.

"Eight bells, my love. If you're late I'll have you keel-hauled."

By the time I presented myself the crew were already assembled by the main hatch. Joshua had his Bible open, prepared to read. I occupied myself with studying the square set of his shoulders and the way the sun touched his fair hair to gold.

> "They that go down to the sea in ships,
> That do business in great waters,
> These see the works of the Lord,
> And his wonders in the deep."

Wasn't that the same psalm he had read on the first voyage? I hoped he didn't mean to repeat himself every Sunday.

> "For he commandeth, and raiseth the stormy
>   wind,
> Which lifteth up the waves thereof.
> They mount up to the heaven,
> They go down again to the depths."

A vision of gigantic Cape Horn greybeards reared up before me, blotting out the peaceful Sunday sky. I shuddered. The horror of those waves still lay ahead of us.

"Their soul is melted because of trouble.
They reel to and fro,
and stagger like a drunken man
And are at their wit's end."

That's what I had been, all right. At my wit's end. Had
Joshua ever really known what it was to be afraid? He said he
had. I remembered the confession he had made to me on that
hill where we were to build our home. The conversation had
unsettled me. I didn't like to think of Joshua needing someone
else—even God. It was like admitting weakness. And then he
had had the nerve to suggest that I needed to know God, too,
and that our marriage wouldn't be complete unless I did. It
was really too much. It was like being asked to be married to
two people instead of one. I wasn't prepared to accept that.

Joshua finished reading the psalm, and I listened critically:

"Then they cry unto the Lord in their trouble,
And he bringeth them out of their distresses.
He maketh the storm a calm, so that the waves
    thereof are still.
Then they are glad because they be quiet:
So he bringeth them unto their desired haven."

As soon as he finished the service, I pounced on him. "God
didn't help Andrew very much, did he?" Joshua shrugged.

"I think he did."

"How can you say that!"

"Mary, we weren't there. We don't know what happened.
But I believe your brother would have called out to the Lord,
just like that sailor in the psalm. And I believe God took him
out of his distress."

I shook my head incredulously. "Are you calling death a
haven?"

"Not death, but what lies beyond it. I don't pretend to know all the answers, but I accept the ones God has given us in this book." He looked down at the battered volume in his hands. "I wish you'd read them for yourself. Just for the sake of argument, of course."

"Maybe sometime I will, captain! Just for the sake of argument. But I'd still much rather sleep in on Sunday mornings."

I should have known better than to expect sloth to be tolerated on any ship of Joshua's. My days were soon scheduled from beginning to end with washing, cleaning, mending, and extra cooking for the crew. Joshua encouraged me to take the sights and work up our position every now and then, just to keep in practice, but I did it without much enthusiasm. Taking the sights meant contact with Mr. Keeler that I would rather avoid. Not that he ever actually said or did anything to offend: it was his attitude of veiled amusement toward everyone and his watchfulness that bothered me. As if he knew something the rest of us didn't.

One afternoon as I came up from the cabin the sound of laughter far up the foredeck attracted my attention. I saw that one of the off-duty hands, not having any luck fishing, had tossed his baited line onto the deck and waited for some greedy seagull to take it. One had, of course, swallowing the hook and effectively tying himself to the sailor. I watched his tormentor. The man allowed the bird enough line to take to the air, then jerked him cruelly backward again. It was all I could do not to rush forward and cut the line myself. Then I noticed Keeler leaning against the rail not ten feet from me. He was smiling.

"Don't you see what's going on down there?"

"I see it well enough, ma'am."

"Well? Why don't you do something!" I shouted, frustrated.

"The lad's only having a little harmless fun. It's just a filthy gull."

"Mr. Keeler, I demand that you put a stop to it—at once. Or I'll do it myself."

He laughed and drawled, "We can't have that, can we? What would the captain think?"

"*About what, mister?*"

Joshua came from around the corner of the after house and I rushed at him. "Joshua, please! Do something. That bird—" I pointed. "They're torturing him. I can't stand it."

His face darkened as he took in the situation. He snapped, "Get that line cut, Keeler. Look lively about it."

"Aye, sir."

The mate moved off, and Joshua stopped him.

"Just one thing more, mister. I don't go in for that kind of thing on this ship. If the men can't find something better to do with their time I'll find something for them. Is that understood?"

The mate paused only momentarily. "Understood, captain."

In a moment the seagull was cut free and fluttered off to settle on the waves. We were near enough, when we passed him, to see the dark flecks of blood on the white feathers.

I choked, "He'll die, won't he? How could they do such a thing?"

"Don't think about it, Mary."

It was the look on the mate's face that had most disturbed me.

"Mr. Keeler laughed when I asked him to interfere."

"I'm afraid there aren't many seamen who would see anything wrong with baiting a gull."

"But it's cruel!"

He sighed. "Most of those men have known more deliberate cruelty under mates and skippers. That doesn't excuse them, but it may help you to understand."

"Well, I don't understand. You didn't turn hard and unfeeling. I think some people are just born mean. Like Mr. Keeler."

"I have no complaints about Mr. Keeler."

"Why do the men act like they're afraid of him?"

"He keeps them in line. If he's been heavy-handed with the discipline a time or two, it's because they're a rough lot. I told you that."

"I've watched him," I said ominously. "He enjoys throwing his weight around and ordering unnecessary duties."

"Mary, obviously you don't like the man, but let's not make him into a villain. As long as he keeps this ship running smoothly Mr. Keeler will have my support."

But the ship was not running smoothly. What reason could there be for the slow progress we were making? The *Car* was in excellent trim and the wind was at our back. During our first few days at sea she had easily put her rival, the *Intrepid*, under her stern. Now, however, I saw Joshua frown as he logged the distance for each twenty-four hour period. At speeds of sixteen and seventeen knots we should be making well over three hundred miles, yet we were falling far short.

On deck Joshua kept a relentless eye on sky, seas and sail. Whenever the log line was run out he waited tensely for the verdict, ready to brace yards or jockey sails at anything less than seventeen knots. Sometimes he took the helm himself to feel if the ship was properly balanced. I was reminded of a musician, making himself one with the instrument that he tuned. It took all of my persuasion each evening to get him to quit the deck.

"A man has no business taking a wife if he's already married to the sea!" I complained one night as I got ready for bed. "You don't know I'm alive half the time."

He snuck up behind me and seized me around the waist. "What about the other half?" I struggled half-heartedly.

"I wish I knew where you got all your energy."

"Must be all that fresh air." He kissed the nape of my neck. "We had a good day today, Mary my love. Touched eighteen knots. If this wind holds we'll soon be running up to the *Romance of the Seas*."

"There's always an 'if,' isn't there? Funny, the *Neptune* never does as well when you're not on deck. It's as if she's jealous of the little time I have you." My arms encircled his neck, drawing his face down to mine. Suddenly he stiffened.

"Joshua? What's wrong?"

"What you said, about the ship not doing so well when I'm below. It's true."

"Don't be absurd, Joshua. I was just joking!"

"If the *Neptune* held to the same speeds we'd be covering between three-fifty and four hundred miles a day instead of just scraping three. Read the log slate. She slows every time I'm not there."

"You don't really think you have some magic power over her, do you?"

"Of course not," he said impatiently. "And I don't think the wind drops every time I walk away, either. If this ship isn't doing her best it's because she's not being handled right by those in charge."

"Mr. Keeler and Hare, your second mate?"

He nodded. "They're the officers of the watch."

"But you've told me a dozen times how good they are!"

"Maybe they need a little prodding." He reached for his jacket and I cried, "Where are you going?"

"Just for a turn around the deck. I won't be long."

"Oh, you won't, will you? Well, just don't expect me to be waiting up when you get back!"

He laughed, caught me as I started to flounce away and pulled me against his chest.

When he returned about an hour later I was still awake. "Everything all right?"

"You must have heard that main royal blow. I kept aft, out of sight, to see what Keeler would do."

"And?"

"Just as I thought," he glared at me. "He didn't order another one sent up."

"Most men in their right minds wouldn't! Do you know how much canvas you've split in the last two weeks? You have our poor sailmaker working night and day."

"That isn't my concern. Driving this ship is. Keeler should know that by now."

"I'm sure you made that clear to him beyond any shadow of a doubt. Now, let's forget about Mr. Keeler, shall we?"

I suppose it was a major achievement on my part that he did forget, at least for a while. It was only in the early hours of the morning, when the thunder of another burst sail momentarily roused me, that I was aware that he had once more slipped away.

chapteR 16

After another few days the question of how much canvas to crowd onto our top hamper became moot. The wind let go, leaving sails slack and tempers almost as hot as the equatorial sun above us. The doldrums. I had forgotten how hideously uncomfortable they could be.

"Have you noticed," I said as we picked at our Saturday luncheon, "that Doc has a curious habit of repeating menus according to what day it is? Monday breakfast it's tripe, Wednesday noon it's dry hash and Friday supper you can count on soup and tinned mutton."

"There's nothing wrong in following a routine. At least there are no surprises."

"I like surprises. Routine is *boring*, Joshua. Just once I'd like to sit down to a Saturday night supper without knowing we were going to have baked beans and brown bread."

"It's the heat," Joshua said indulgently. "You'll get over it."

"Heat!" I muttered as he went off. Manolo picked up the dishes, humming cheerfully.

"What do you think, Manolo?"

"*Qué?* I do not understand, señora."

"Don't pretend you weren't listening. What do you think about Doc's cooking?"

He shrugged. "Is good, señora."

"I want your help, Manolo. We need a change, something to cheer us up."

I tapped my fingers on the table while he watched warily.

"Chicken! That's it. We still have plenty in the coop. Tell Doc tonight's supper is to be fresh chicken with rice and vegetables, and for dessert a dried-apple pie!" My mouth watered, thinking about it.

Manolo shook his head. "He will not like that, señora."

"It won't hurt Doc to put in a little extra effort."

"It is not him. It is the captain who will not like it."

"Fiddlesticks. Of course he will, he loves chicken."

But I was less sure of myself as the afternoon wore on. The breathless heat was putting everyone on edge. Delicate breezes, known as "cat's paws," pushed us along only a few yards every now and then. Then a fist fight broke out between two of the men. Joshua instructed the mate to set them to tarring the rigging—one of the least-favorite chores. One sailor, a German, told Mr. Keeler in loud and colorful language what he thought of the idea, and Keeler struck him.

Then it all happened quickly. With horror I saw the German pull a knife, saw Mr. Keeler moving with lighting speed to knock the man unconscious. And then it was over. Or so I thought, until the mate ordered the sailor triced up to the mainmast.

"Joshua." I clutched his arm. "What's he going to do?"

"Nothing," he said, raising his voice. "*Mr. Keeler!* Cut that man down and put him in the brig."

"Aye, I'll cut the dog down! After he gets the beating he deserves!"

"*Now*, Mr. Keeler."

Even from a distance I could see the fury on the mate's face. Then he snapped out an order and walked away.

"He was going to flog that man!"

"That's the usual punishment when a crew member threatens an officer."

"But you stopped him. Why? Was it for my sake?"

"It's not something I'd like you to witness. But that isn't why. I don't believe in flogging. I've seen too many bloodied backs not to know it does little good—either for the man punished or the man who's applying the punishment. Discipline, yes. But without humiliation, or you'll have a crew that hates you more than it fears you."

"I think Mr. Keeler hates you, for interfering."

He shrugged. "He'll get over it."

But I knew the incident had disturbed him. It was not Joshua's practice to come between his mate's exercise of authority with the crew, nor had it ever been necessary with our previous mate, Mr. Buckley. I had a strong feeling that Mr. Keeler would not be the type to forgive or forget.

As suppertime drew near I told myself that a little festivity was exactly what was needed to lift our spirits. I dressed up in a flounced pink gown that was one of Joshua's favorites and spent an hour brushing and twisting my hair into one of the elaborate chignons I had seen the ladies wear in New York. When Joshua joined me in the saloon he looked at me blankly.

"What's the occasion?"

"No special occasion. I just felt like looking beautiful for my husband."

"Pretty fancy rig for Saturday night beans," he grunted. "What did you do to your hair?"

"It's the newest fashion. Don't you like it?"

"I liked it better the way it was."

"Oh honestly, Joshua. What a stick-in-the-mud!"

Manolo sidled in that moment with a platter of chicken. He set it down in front of Joshua and then scurried away. My stomach fluttered nervously.

"What's this?" Joshua said, staring at the platter. "*Chicken?*"

"Why, so it is."

"This is Saturday night. We always have baked beans and brown bread on Saturday night."

"I know, but—"

"*Steward! Look alive when I call you, mister!*"

Manolo edged around the corner from the pantry. He cast me a panic-stricken glance.

"What's the meaning of this, sir?"

"Of what, señor captain?"

"This *chicken!* What else?"

The steward grinned feebly and shrugged.

"Tell Doc to report to me. We'll get to the bottom of it."

"Joshua. It wasn't Doc's idea, or Manolo's. It was mine."

There was a deadly silence. Manolo sneaked away.

"I thought I had made it quite clear before, Mary, that I do not approve of your meddling with the ship's routine."

"If you could only hear yourself!" I tried to giggle, but it did not help my cause. "All of this tempest over a—a pile of beans!"

He tried to maintain his dignity. "I happen to like beans. Besides, it's the principle. They're a time-honored tradition."

"Poor Joshua. A trying day and now this. I suppose you won't want any of the apple pie Doc made for dessert, either."

"Apple pie?"

"We could save it for tomorrow. Or isn't it traditional to eat apple pie on Sunday?"

His eyes narrowed. "I know a tacking maneuver when I see one. Trying to get me to alter course, are you, woman?"

"My dearest captain. You did that the day you married me. You just haven't realized it yet."

I would not very often get away with it, but time-honored tradition was thrown, for that one night at least, to the nonexistent winds. My husband was stubborn, but he was not stupid. He took full pleasure in the chicken and the dessert and whatever else his lady was inclined to offer. It was a most satisfactory evening.

Unfortunately, the euphoria did not last. My energy evaporated as one hot day succeeded another, with only the lightest of breezes to move us slowly through the equatorial zone. I lay about in a deck chair, irritable and bored. One morning Joshua suggested I take the altitude sights while he went below and checked the chronometer. Mr. Keeler was assigned to record my findings.

Whether it was the mate's uncomfortable proximity or the terrible intensity of the sun's rays, I don't know, but suddenly my vision blurred and wavered. I swayed and would have dropped the sextant had Mr. Keeler not grabbed it.

"I'm sorry," I gasped. "It's this heat."

"I'll take over." He gripped my arm and though I recoiled from his touch I was too dizzy to shake it off. He steered me to a canopy-shaded chair.

"You won't mention this to the captain, I hope? He'd be furious if anything happened to that sextant."

"I won't if you don't want me to." His dark eyes mocked mine, and then wandered deliberately over the rest of me. I flushed with impotent fury. As soon as he had finished with the sextant, I took it below to escape his presence.

"I don't know what's got into you lately," Joshua said later on. "You're as prickly as a sea urchin. When Keeler spoke to you at lunch you nearly bit off his head."

"I don't like the man."

"That's plain enough. But as long as he's my first officer I'll thank you to keep a civil tongue when you address him."

I burst into tears. "Everything's always my fault!"

"Has he ever treated you with discourtesy?"

"He—he looks at me sometimes!"

"Really? So does every man on this ship."

"It's the way he looks at me. As if—"

"Yes?"

"Oh, I can't explain it. But when he says something to me, I know he's really *thinking* something else."

"Mary." Joshua's voice took on the long-suffering tone that always infuriated me. "Isn't it just possible that you are imagining a little bit of this? You sound exactly like one of the heroines in those romantic novels you're so fond of reading."

"I knew you'd say that! You think I'm making the whole thing up, don't you?"

"It's understandable. The heat, being the only woman aboard the ship—it's bound to be difficult. All I'm asking is that you restrain yourself from open warfare with Keeler. The crew can sense things like that and it's not good for the morale."

I subsided. It was no use talking with Joshua, he simply couldn't understand my growing feeling of apprehension. And how could he, when I couldn't fully explain it to myself?

In the South Atlantic we ran into a series of thunderstorms. They gave Joshua the winds he was looking for and sent me quivering to my berth, convinced that every fork of lighting was aimed at our destruction. More often than not, it seemed to me, I would wake in the darkness and find his place beside me empty. I was angry and hurt. I thought only of my own distress, and nothing of his concern that we were falling further and further behind in our schedule.

Then one day he came bursting into our quarters, raving that he had discovered his first mate asleep on his watch.

"I wouldn't have believed it unless I saw it with my own eyes. Of course, he swore up and down it wasn't true. But he was *sitting down* on a deck chair, Mary!"

"Well, sitting isn't the same thing as sleeping."

"I have never sat down while on duty during all my years at sea! It just isn't done, not even by a captain, if he's worth his salt."

I shrugged. "Not everyone shares your standards, my dear."

"Everyone on *my* ship will, or he can sling his hammock somewhere else! I told Keeler if I ever caught him swinging the lead again it would be the last time."

"So you have given him another chance? I'm surprised."

"I need him," he said simply. "The second mate is a good man, but he hasn't had enough training or experience to manage the crew. And I'm going to need everything I can get out of them at the Horn."

"Will it be as bad this time, do you think?"

"Worse." He added, noting my expression, "I'm sorry, but you may as well be prepared. It's the wrong time of year for the Horn. The seasons are reversed, so it's winter there now. A Cape Horn winter is not something I relish."

Several mornings later we hailed a vessel bound for Rio and received a confirmation of just how bad things were ahead of us. The captain, shouting through his horn, told us he was headed in for repairs. His men had been at the pumps around the clock.

"Worst rounding I seen in years—and I seen plenty of dirty weather, believe me! You better think twice if you figure you're going to make any headway against those westerlies. You're sailin' the wrong way, mister!"

The grim warning might have succeeded in deflecting other men, but not Joshua. His resolve only grew a little stiffer. Though he would not admit it, I knew he looked forward to the battle ahead as an exhilarating challenge to be met and conquered. The possibility of defeat never even entered his mind.

However, the sense of foreboding that had shadowed me during the last weeks now took on a definite form and substance. I was convinced that we were heading into grave danger, perhaps the worst we had ever faced.

chapter
17

After the exchange with the captain of the damaged vessel, Joshua seemed to spend more and more time on deck. He seemed obsessed with the need to cover greater distances before we were stalled by bad weather. And he was now practically certain Mr. Keeler was shortening sail without reason.

"Why would he want to do that?" I asked patiently. Joshua was sitting at his charts, his brow furrowed as he studied our course. My mending lay untouched on my lap. I wished tiredly that our conversation did not always have to center around the first mate or the *Neptune's Car* or anything else having to do with the sea or sailing. I wished things between us could be as they were during those trouble-free summer days in Maine, overlooking Penobscot Bay.

"Why? That's what I'd like to know. Keeler never struck me as the cautious type."

"Maybe he just likes defying you when he gets the chance. He probably fancies himself a better skipper."

"Maybe." He pondered that. "But that's risky, and

Keeler's smart for all his superior airs. I think he may have another reason for slowing us down."

"Such as?"

"Such as being in the pay of someone who would benefit by it. Someone with heavy money on either the *Intrepid* or *Romance of the Seas.*"

I blinked. "You're talking about sabotage?"

"It's possible. There's a lot of money wrapped up in clipper races. I would be surprised if most of the sailors on this vessel haven't made wagers of some sort."

"But you have no proof?"

"No. And I may be very wrong. All the same, I intend to keep a close watch on Mr. Keeler."

The situation was bound to have its effect. Joshua was remote, distracted by his concern for the ship. Mealtimes that we shared with Mr. Keeler became a trial to be endured. Suspicion, I found, was a poisonous thing, coloring even the most innocent words and behavior. I began to dread my encounters with the mate more than ever, and he, amused, seemed to sense it.

As we approached the fortieth parallel the temperature took a sudden plunge. I woke one morning feeling ill, and used the excuse to stay in bed and read all day. Manolo loved to pamper me. He brought lunch and dinner trays heaped with food which, oddly enough, I had no trouble consuming.

"Cape Horn fever," Joshua diagnosed that evening. "If you were one of my crew you'd do double duty for that stunt."

"But I did feel sick this morning, Joshua, truly I did!"

"Nerves. Keep busy, that's the best cure. I don't want to have to worry about you along with everything else. Understood?"

"Oh, aye, aye, captain," I sulked, "perfectly!"

The next morning the nausea attacked again. I managed to control it until Joshua went up on deck, and then was violently sick. Manolo brought me tea, looking concerned.

"You want me to ask the captain for some medicine, señora?"

"*No!*" I said fiercely. "I forbid you to say a word to him!"

"But, señora—"

"I will *not* be accused of having an attack of vapors. Besides, it's not necessary. I feel better already."

The steward went away, shaking his head. Feeling defiant, I plunged into a rigorous cleaning of the cabin, emptying and arranging drawers, polishing furniture. The longer I worked, the better I felt. I was forced, reluctantly, to concede the effectiveness of Joshua's cure. Perhaps it was nerves, after all. Perhaps if I could keep busy enough I could rid myself entirely of the fears that haunted me.

Dense fogs and icy rain greeted our entry into the roaring forties. Joshua, realizing he needed to conserve his energies for the struggles ahead of him, finally resorted to padlocking the halyards and left the deck. The officer of the watch was to fetch him only when he judged it absolutely necessary to reduce sail.

I was not surprised that Joshua slept like a stone that night. I myself was not so fortunate. I woke uncomfortably aware of being flung against Joshua on one side and the raised edge of the berth on the other. The *Neptune's Car* was rearing frantically; the wind, only of modest strength a few hours before, was lifting its voice in a banshee howl. The storm had come up quickly, as they often did in this region. I contemplated my sleeping husband with uncertainty. Should I wake him? He needed the rest so badly, and yet I was uneasy. The clipper was carrying her royals, and that was too much sail. Why hadn't the mate called him?

A deafening report from aloft suddenly ended the debate. Joshua shot out of bed, grabbing for his clothes.

"What are those fools about up there?" He flung on his weather gear and raced for the door. Before he reached it we both heard, like the crack of doom, another sail sacrificed to the winds.

Somebody, I thought grimly, is going to pay for this night. And I had a very strong hunch who that someone was.

It was much later before Joshua could tell me what had happened. When he found the mate, he said, he was sheltered in the lee, watching with apparent unconcern while the crew worked to gather the blown-out canvas.

"Are you mad, mister," he shouted, "or do you want to see us dismasted?"

"I wasn't the one who locked the halyards, *sir*."

Joshua's fist connected squarely with the mate's jaw. Keeler dropped like lead onto the deck.

"*Stefenack!*"

The third mate ran aft. "Aye, sir?"

"Call all hands and rally in those topgallants. Double-reef fore and main tops'ls. Lively, now!"

"Aye, aye, captain!"

"And ask Mr. Hare to report to me."

Men surged onto the yardarms. Mr. Hare, the second mate, was on the quarterdeck inside two minutes. He sent an astonished look at the crumpled form of his superior.

Joshua said tersely, "Do you want to tell me what's going on here, Mr. Hare?"

"I wish I knew, sir."

"Are you going to pretend the wind wasn't beginning to blow up before your watch changed?"

"It was, sir, I won't deny it. But it was nowhere near a gale. I figured I could hold on to the canvas at least till Mr.

Keeler relieved me. Knew for sure he'd start haulin' in and clewin' up."

"But he didn't."

"No, sir." The second mate looked puzzled. "It don't make sense, him not fetchin' you. I seen him order in sail when there was no need for it."

"And you said nothing?"

His shoulders lifted. "Would be like whistlin' psalms to the taffrail, cap'n. Mr. Keeler has no use for me nor anyone else on this ship."

"You should have come to me."

"And caught a bloody skull for goin' over his head? With respect, sir, I don't think you know Mr. Keeler very well."

"I know well enough what he did tonight, Mr. Hare, and that's enough. Take him below."

"To his quarters, cap'n?"

"To the brig. And do it double quick before I change my mind and make an example of him."

"Aye, aye, sir!"

It was a long night. Before the *Neptune's Car* was under control another topsail split and we lost a jib. It was well after dawn before Joshua took time to come below and tell me what was going on.

"You should have had that traitor in irons weeks ago," I commented as I poured out coffee and served him an early breakfast. "At least now you won't have to wonder what he's doing behind your back! What will you do about replacing him? Advance Mr. Hare?"

"No."

"Then who will stand his watch?"

He took a gulp of his coffee. "I will."

"Joshua—"

"I won't allow any more leeway for incompetence."

"We're at least a week from Cape Horn, maybe two. Am I right?"

He didn't answer.

"You seriously believe you can stand the first watch, supervise the second, plus do all the navigation until we've doubled the Horn?"

"I've survived double watches before," he growled.

"But for how long? Joshua, be sensible. Who knows how long we'll have to stand off before we can make westing?"

He set his mug down and stood up. "Thanks for the coffee. It's time to relieve Hare."

"Oh! You are the stubbornest man I've ever known!"

"And you, my dear, are the stubbornest, most irresistible woman. Especially in that nightgown." He kissed me. "Go back to bed."

"Can't I persuade you to come with me?"

"You can. That's why I'm going to cut and run, before I'm aground!"

He left. I remained at the table, despondently reflecting that I would probably be spending a great deal of time alone in the near future. Duty before pleasure, that was Joshua.

I looked at the remains of his hurried breakfast: a platter of fatty potatoes, bacon wallowing in grease, and eggs that stared at me with doleful yellow eyes, daring me to puncture them. The bile rose in my throat.

"*Manolo!*"

The steward appeared from the pantry. "Sí, señora?"

"I feel so—get me a—" I groaned, covered my mouth, and fled. He followed after a few moments, by which time I had already emptied my stomach of its contents and collapsed on the settee.

"You sick again, señora?"

"Whatever gave you that idea?"

"I think maybe it is right I tell the captain. Sí?"

"No!" I sat up. "You may not tell him, especially not now! He has too much on his mind." I giggled weakly. "Maybe all I need is a dose of your cayenne pepper!"

He shook his head. "You are not seasick, señora."

"Oh? I suppose you think you know the cause of my mysterious malady?"

"Sí, señora. Many times I have seen my Margueretta behave so."

"Well? Out with it! I'm not going to die, am I?" I laughed.

"Oh, no señora! It is cause for much joy! The señora is with child."

I felt the color drain from my face. "What?"

"A little one! You are to become a *mamacita!*"

"That is not very funny, Manolo. In fact, I think it's quite crude of you to suggest such a thing."

He looked bewildered. "You do not wish to become a *mamacita?*"

"Stop saying that word!" I shouted. "The whole thing is preposterous. I am not expecting a baby. I couldn't be."

The steward shrugged and went out, closing the door softly.

It was ridiculous, I told myself again. I got up and went to the looking glass. I looked the same as I always had. A trifle pale, perhaps, but that was to be expected. I ran my hands slowly down my waist. I had gained a few pounds, but I often did when I was nervous and overeating. Couldn't the same reason explain the other departures from my normal physical functioning? Surely, I thought, I would have sensed it if my own body housed a life beside my own.

And then I began to tremble. I remembered the recurrent distress that Victoria had suffered during the early months of her pregnancy. Other details came to mind. I examined each one in the light of this new, overwhelming possibility. Gradually uncertainty evolved into a conviction.

"It's true. It's true! Oh, Joshua!"

For a long while I just sat hugging my wonder and delight to myself. Then I got up and hurriedly, eagerly, pulled on my clothes. Joshua would be beside himself. I couldn't wait to tell him, to see the look on his face. I drew a heavy wool cloak around my shoulders and ran toward the companion door. Then I stopped.

The memory of those dark, bitter days in Hong Kong fell over me, obscuring the joy. I had once deceived Joshua into thinking I carried his child. What if I should deceive him again, even innocently? Other women had made mistakes about such things. If I were wrong—I drew a deep, shuddering breath. No, I must not be wrong. I must never risk hurting Joshua again.

Another thought came to me. Would it be wise—even if I were absolutely certain of my condition—to choose this particular time to tell him? The next few weeks would call for every bit of Joshua's skill and concentration. It would be unfair to add to the burden of his responsibilities. Better—far better—for me to wait, until we were safely around the Horn.

Under ordinary circumstances such a resolve would have been useless. Joshua had an uncanny way of knowing if I kept something from him, and *this* secret was all but bursting from me. But we saw little of each other during the following storm-filled days. Joshua would remain on deck until it was no longer possible to keep his eyes open. When he came below it was only to swallow an all-too-hasty meal and stretch himself on our berth for a few hours' rest.

I helped as much as I could with the navigating. Every so often, hungry for his presence, I would put on oilskins and fight my way to his side on deck. We couldn't talk but I liked to believe it made some difference to him for me to be there.

It was all I could do to keep my balance, hanging on the braces. Seas broke over the lower decks so constantly that the wash ports were lashed open to keep water draining through the scuppers. It was a fearful sight. And the glass was dropping. I knew the flying spray would soon turn everything it touched to ice.

Once, during a lull in the wind, Joshua pointed out a speck of white off the starboard bow, rising to the crest of each wave and then disappearing into the valleys.

"See him? An albatross, sleeping with his head tucked under his wings!"

I shook my head in amazement. "How can any creature sleep in the midst of all this fury?"

Joshua smiled. It was one of the things I loved about him, his sensitivity toward all living things. I knew now that it was often the strongest men who were the most tender.

"If I were an artist, I'd paint that. I'd call the picture 'perfect peace.'"

The bird slept on until our approach disturbed him. He stared at us, then stretched his great wings and lifted majestically into the air. With a sudden change of mood Joshua inquired whimsically, "Did I every tell you that albatrosses are supposed to harbor the souls of sea captains who go down off Cape Horn?"

I suppressed a shiver. "What a revolting superstition. What happens to their wives?"

"Ah! What else could they turn into but those squawking Cape pigeons?"

Such exchanges became increasingly rare, however. Sleeplessness and constant exposure to the cold began to take their toll. I ached, seeing Joshua's exhilaration take on a plodding determination that could only, inevitably, lead to exhaustion. I tried to reason with him.

"If you make yourself sick, then what?"

"You worry too much."

"How can I help it? Look at you. You don't eat enough, your eyes are so bloodshot they can hardly focus. You're a man, Joshua, not some kind of super-being."

"*Stow it, will you?*"

I flinched, and he closed his eyes. "I'm sorry, Mary. I didn't mean to raise my voice. But this is how things have to be right now. Don't make it harder."

I didn't say any more, but I wanted to. A sudden, intense yearning possessed me to share with my husband the news that could wipe some of the weariness from his face, and give him gladness. But it would be wrong. Concern for me would overbalance the joy, add even more stress. To blurt out my secret now would do more harm than good.

There was plenty to keep me occupied. I treated frostbite, chilblains, the torn and bloodied fingers of the crew as they coped with their work in the savage cold. Sails froze into sheet metal. Squalls of sleet drove into exposed flesh like hot needles. The decks were covered with drifts.

Latitude 54°43', Longitude 65°23'. We sighted Staten Island. Joshua doubled the lookouts and I knew that they watched for the pale, spectral forms of drifting ice that could crush a ship to splinters. Ice everywhere, around us and above us. Men were sent aloft to chip the frozen weight of it from the yardarms. Ice around my heart, as Joshua steered for the Strait of Le Maire.

He said it was the only way to make westing, but he was nearly at the end of his physical strength. Only his spirit whipped him on, telling him he could do the impossible. When he was unable to stand long hours he lashed himself into a chair and then drove the *Neptune's Car* through the gales and mountainous seas. Somehow, miraculously, we made it through the Strait.

I lay on my berth that night listening to the disappointed shriek of the wind. *Now,* I thought, perhaps now he will let someone take over for him, and rest. I lay for a long time waiting for him, hoping. And then I fell asleep.

chapter
18

A loud disturbance on the companionway woke me. I sat up groggily. Could it be Joshua? No, it was someone heavier, staggering. Then someone shouted my name and I ran to throw open the door.

The second mate stood there swaying. A man lay slung over his shoulders.

"I found the cap'n like this, ma'am, still strapped to his chair. I don't know how long—"

"Dear God!" I breathed, stepping back into the cabin. "Lay him on the bed. Quickly!"

Following the mate into the bedroom I helped him stretch out Joshua's unconscious form. Then I began at once to strip away the clothing that clung, half frozen to his body.

"Got any brandy, ma'am?"

"No—yes. There's some in the medicine chest, under the cupboard. Manolo knows where."

He went off. I took a towel and rubbed the stiffened limbs briskly, trying to restore circulation. When the mate returned we heaped warm layers of blankets over Joshua. Then we tried to force down some of the fiery liquid from the flask.

Joshua coughed and choked, mumbling something incoherent.

"Now what, Mr. Hare?"

The big man looked helpless. "I reckon you've had more experience doctorin' than me, ma'am."

"Cuts and bruises and broken bones! Nothing like this!" With a convulsive movement Joshua threw off his quilts. As I pulled them back on I threw a glance over my shoulder.

"I expect you need to be getting back to the quarterdeck, Mr. Hare."

"Aye, ma'am." He started away and then paused. "Ma'am? Don't you worry 'bout the old man. He's tough. He'll weather it."

I felt a surge of gratitude toward the gruff, red-bearded sailor. Of course he was right. Joshua was only exhausted. His body had been forced beyond endurance and it had finally shut down. I would give him the care and rest he needed.

I crept into bed beside Joshua and drew him close, like a child, seeking to convey my body's warmth. Gradually he became less restive.

"My stubborn, invincible captain," I whispered, "you are made of flesh and blood after all. Your clipper is going to have to get along without you for a while."

The bell on deck struck eight times. Four o'clock. Who would stand Joshua's watch for him? I would have to send for the second mate and discuss the matter.... My eyelids drooped. When they jerked open, a few hours later, Joshua was shouting and thrashing in delirium. His face was fiery hot.

I scrambled from the bed, rebuking myself bitterly. Why hadn't I stayed awake? Watched over him? Wringing out a cloth I bathed Joshua's face, wondering desperately what to do. Could the fever be pneumonia? It was not an unlikely possibility. And it was, at least, something I had dealt with.

Manolo knocked. "I wake and hear the captain shouting. You need me?"

"I'm afraid Captain Patten is ill, Manolo. Find some flannel and tear it into strips for a poultice."

While the poultice was being prepared I got out the medicine chest. I could not endure to see Joshua in such pain. I picked up one after another of the vials and read the spidery scrawl on each label: *belladonna, dandelion, digitalis, tincture of opium.* . . . I bit my lip, remembering Joshua's distaste for the painkiller. And yet he had given it to me when I was in so much pain, that once. Surely he would allow its use during an emergency such as this?

I looked up the table of medicines in the back of the *Sailor's Guide to Health.*

Opium Pulvis, or, *Tincture of Opium. A hypnotic remedy used to cause sleep. An anodyne (for relief from pain). 4 to 8 drops.*

With unsteady hands I measured five drops into a glass, stirred in a little water, and held the mixture to Joshua's lips. He drank it thirstily. With tears of relief I saw the drug begin to work, smoothing the pain from his features. Manolo came in and together we soaked the flannel strips in flaxseed oil and wrapped them around Joshua's chest.

"I bring you some breakfast now, señora, sí?"

"No, I couldn't eat. What time is it? Past eight?"

"Sí, the watch has changed. Señor Hare, he says he must talk to you."

"Yes, of course. Poor Mr. Hare. Tell him I'll see him at once."

The mate came, twisting his cap in his great hands and looking uneasy.

"Sorry to be botherin' you, ma'am."

"Don't apologize. Please, sit down. I know how tired you must be, and I want you to know how grateful I am for your taking charge."

"That's just it, ma'am! I ain't got no business takin' charge. Me and Stefenack—that's the third mate—we done the best we could last night, but that ain't good enough. The crew knows I carried the old man belowdecks. They want to know who's runnin' this ship."

"I think that's obvious, Mr. Hare. You are, until the captain is back on his feet."

"And how long is that likely to take, ma'am?"

"I don't know!" I lost control and covered my face with my hands. "Why do you ask me questions I can't answer? Two weeks—three—perhaps more."

"We haven't got weeks." The mate's voice was grim. "We ain't even got that many days to play with. There's no place on God's earth worse than Cape Stiff, and we're smack in the middle of it."

"Well, what do you propose? We can't drag the captain out of his sickbed. You'll have to give the orders."

"I'm just second greaser, ma'am. I don't know nothin' about navigatin'!"

I sat very still. "Are you telling me, Mr. Hare, that other than the captain there is no one aboard this ship who can navigate?"

"There's Mr. Keeler, ma'am."

"*No.* He is not to be considered."

The mate sighed. "Then you'll have to do it, ma'am. There's no one else."

"That's impossible."

"I seen you take the sights."

"Only once in a while—for my own amusement! And Joshua—Captain Patten—always verified my reckonings himself!" I shook my head. "It's out of the question. Even if I were qualified, my first responsibility is to care for my husband."

"Miz Patten. I'm thinkin' the best way you can help him is by sailin' us out o' this hell hole. The quicker the better."

I stared at him as the full import of what he was saying began to penetrate. We were trapped. We had traveled thousands of miles down the South American coast and now, at its very tip, we were caught in the deadly whirlpool between Atlantic and Pacific. And we had no captain.

I got up and walked into the bedroom where Joshua lay sleeping peacefully.

Why? I thought, for the first time feeling anger toward him. *Why did you bring us here, and then leave us to sort it all out? Why did you let yourself get sick? Oh, Joshua—tell me! What should I do?*

I returned slowly to the mate.

"There is one alternative you haven't mentioned. We could turn back to Rio, Mr. Hare. It would be much safer than trying to go west."

"Aye." He inclined his head.

"But you don't think we should?"

"That's not for me to say, ma'am."

"It's what Joshua would say. He'd be furious to find out we'd given up without even a fight!" I tried to smile. "Perhaps facing Cape Horn would be easier."

"By your leave, ma'am, I'll pass the word you'll be layin' our course yourself. Will it be east or west, Miz Patten?"

"*West.* . . . And may God grant we haven't made a mistake, Mr. Hare."

chapter
19

Mr. Hare and I divided the duties between us. Stefenack, he said, was too green to be trusted with a quarterdeck watch. So I would have to stand at least a part of it. Most importantly, I must take the observations necessary for reckoning our position and charting our course. And I would keep the log.

I knew that none of it was going to be easy. I did not, however, guess how much it would cost me to walk away from Joshua while he was in such distress, even for short periods. Manolo was the most reliable of attendants. He was instructed to fetch me for any difficulty at all. But I wanted to be there *myself*—caring for him. Every instinct cried out for it.

On the quarterdeck I knew that I had to push such thoughts aside. Lack of concentration on the winds, the currents, the form and direction of the clouds, could play havoc with a ship at the best of times. During a Cape Horn winter, a mistake would mean death.

Mr. Hare triced up a weather cloth for a lee, but it afforded little protection. The *Neptune's Car* was making heavy weather against the powerful westerlies. What madness was it, I asked myself, that drove men and their vessels to such suicidal lengths to reach California? Nothing could be worth this. *Nothing*.

A ship was sighted, standing off to the southeast. The *Intrepid? Romance of the Seas?* She was too far distant to be identified. Somehow, it no longer seemed important.

I carried the sextant below and did some arithmetic. Our latitude and longitude, I discovered, had not varied significantly from the last entry in the log. That meant that we were not making much progress. On the positive side, it meant the *Neptune's Car* was at least holding her own.

If my calculations were correct. Doubt stung. Of course they were correct! Hadn't I worked out the figures exactly as I had hundreds of times before?

If I'm wrong, if I'm only a few degrees off, we could be bearing straight for the rocks.

I picked up the nautical almanac. Perhaps, to be safe, I should go through it once more.

"Señora?" Manolo appeared at the bedroom door. "The captain calls for you."

"He is conscious?" Hope surged through me. I ran into the next room and saw that his eyes were open.

"Joshua!"

He did not recognize me. I said quietly, "The drug is wearing off. It's all right. I will stay with the captain awhile, Manolo."

It was already dark in the little cabin. Daylight faded only a few hours after noon in this latitude. I lit a lamp, but the light seemed to bother Joshua. He covered his eyes, his face contorted with pain.

I leaned close. "Is it your head, my darling? Does your head ache?"

He moved restlessly, murmuring. I blew out the light.

I think it was during those long hours that followed, sitting there in the darkness, that I felt for the first time how completely alone I was. It was strange. I had always prided myself on being a self-sufficient person—poised and self-confident. Even another Susan B. Anthony. But it's easy to be scornful of weakness when you're surrounded all your life with people who love you and protect you. My family, friends, Joshua—someone had always been there before when things went wrong. I had never had to rely on my own strength. Now, at last, I was finding out what it was to be alone.

The ship's timbers moaned as they strained against the rising wind. A storm was coming. Joshua, seeming to sense the *Neptune's* distress, became more agitated. I decided to give him some more of the medicine, and called Manolo.

"I've got to go up there and see what's going on. Don't leave him, please! I'll be back as soon as I can."

The snow struck my face as I stepped from the companion-way. I gasped and moved over to the helm. It was almost impossible to make out the movement on the yardarms. Mr. Hare spotted me and came aft.

"We're in for it, sure, ma'am. Reg'lar Cape Horn snorter. Mains'ls don't look like they'll hold out much longer."

I nodded. "Call all hands, Mr. Hare."

In moments the off-duty watch were spilling from the deck house, pulling on sou'westers and jackets that hadn't fully dried from the last call. The mate ordered them aloft, but even as he did so a loud crack jerked our faces upward. The main topgallant had split.

"All right lads, some of you lay up on that mainyard and furl before that canvas blows to ribbons!"

The *Neptune's Car* cleaved a giant wave. I hung on helplessly, my senses reeling and my heart pounding with fear. How could men keep their footing on those icy heights aloft?

The two sailors at the wheel fought to keep the clipper from swinging. Suddenly, I saw it—a black wall of water rushing at us, broad on the port bow.

"*Down helm!*"

The men spun the wheel in the direction of the wind. I watched, horrified, as the ship responded too slowly and the great wave reared up above the weather rail. For an instant it hung there, suspended. Then it broke, hurling tons of foaming sea on the decks below. Crew members attempting to haul home the heavy mainsail were knocked off their feet like ragdolls, the buntlines ripped from their hands. The sail shot up and out of control.

It was as if there were some evil conspiracy between the elements. The wind, shrieking in triumph, caught the blowing canvas and tore it from clew to earing, then tossed it into the sea.

"You men there!" Mr. Hare bellowed, his voice a comforting anchor to sanity, "Cut the bolt ropes! The rest of you help haul in that main course!"

Through chest-deep water he and the others pushed to the rail where the mainsail was still attached. By superhuman effort they managed to drag it back aboard.

The bell for the change of watch went unheeded as all hands settled into the job of hauling down and clewing up. It was an exhausting, miserable business and the weather did nothing to help. The *Car* ran on with her deck at a 45 degree angle, her lee rail under water. By midnight she was down to close-reefed topsails and staysails. The off-duty watch staggered below to catch a few hours sleep, and Mr. Hare came aft to take my place.

I felt as though I could never be warm, or safe, or untroubled ever again. Manolo brought me hot tea, then I tumbled into bed. Joshua never even knew that I was there.

It was the next morning, returning from the four to eight o'clock watch, that I found the letter under the door. It was from Mr. Keeler.

"I don't suppose you know anything about this?" I asked Manolo after scanning it briefly and throwing it on the desk.

The steward looked blank. "What is it, señora?"

"Nothing important, really. Just a friendly greeting from our deposed mate suggesting we let bygones be bygones."

I sank down wearily on the sofa and watched from the corner of my eye as Manolo edged closer to the desk. I knew he had read the note when he burst into a five-minute series of expletives—in Spanish, of course.

"He is swine, señora! He is not fit to wipe your feet on! Why do you not let Manolo take care of señor Keeler? He will not trouble you or the señor captain again!"

"I thank you for your loyalty, my friend. But even you must admit that some of Mr. Keeler's points are true. I haven't much experience sailing a clipper ship. I am only nineteen, and, quite obviously, a female. That in itself is sufficient to damn me in the eyes of the crew. Perhaps it *is* presumptuous of me to take the responsibility for their lives."

"What are you saying, señora? You wish for that man to take over for you?"

I shook my head. "You may give him my answer, if you like. Tell Mr. Keeler that while I appreciate his generous and unselfish offer, I must decline. Since Captain Patten found him unfit to serve as first officer of this vessel, I would hardly think he would approve of naming him commander."

"*Sí, sí,* señora!" The steward grinned. "I tell him, *con mucho gusto!*"

I went softly into the adjoining room. Joshua's eyes were still closed. A strand of hair had fallen across his forehead. I brushed it back and then snatched away my fingers as though they had touched a stove lid. He was burning up with fever—worse, if anything, than before. If this was an inflammation of the lungs he was not responding to treatment.

I sent Manolo for ice and for the next few hours we worked to bring down Joshua's temperature. It was as it another strength took over from my own. The hollowness of hunger and fatigue and the storm that reared around us did not exist. Only Joshua existed, and my determination to make him respond. At last, just before it was time for me to return to the deck watch, Joshua showed signs of returning to consciousness.

"Thank God! We have to keep him from sinking back at all costs, Manolo. Watch him very carefully."

"Sí, señora!"

"Perhaps you can get him to take some broth after a bit." I paused from buttoning up my foul weather gear. "I hate to leave him. But what else can I do? Mr. Hare has to go off duty sometime."

"And you, señora?" Manolo asked somberly. "You, too, need to rest and eat."

"And so I shall. The barometer's stopped falling. I believe things are going to take a turn for the better, Manolo."

The third mate nodded as I came up. Was I imagining it, or did his eyes slide away from mine just now, as though he wished to avoid contact? I studied Mr. Stefenack's profile. It seemed to me there was a lessening of the friendliness that I had seen there before. As the afternoon wore on I became certain. The chill I felt in the air had nothing to do with the temperature.

"It's not just Mr. Stefenack, either," I told Mr. Hare when

he returned for the dog watch. "I've caught several of the men glancing my way when they didn't think I was watching—and then at each other."

His broad shoulders lifted and fell. "Ain't heard no scuttlebut, ma'am. Any blows my way I'll let you know."

"I'd appreciate that, Mr. Hare."

Below, Manolo was attempting to spoon chicken soup into Joshua.

"Good *sopa*, señora. I make it myself!"

"It smells marvelous."

"The señor captain does not like it," he said sadly. "It make him sick. He throw up."

"Oh, well, we'll just have to try again tomorrow. The captain must take nourishment."

"The señora, she would like some of Manolo's *sopa?*"

"Very definitely, *sí!*"

He brought me a large steaming bowl and watched delightedly while I consumed it hungrily.

"Now you are warm inside, señora, I bring you supper. Doc makes it for you."

"Lovely. But it's still early for supper—I'll work on the charts for an hour or so."

My intentions were good, but I had not reckoned on the exhaustion that engulfed me the moment I sat down. Try as I might to throw it off, the weight of my lids grew heavier, the lines and numerals before me more blurred. I cradled my head on my arms and allowed the greybeard of sleep to curl over me.

"*Miz Patten? Miz Patten, it's Hare, ma'am.*"

"What?" I jerked awake, staring around me in bewilderment. The cabin was in darkness, except for a stream of light coming from the room where Manolo sat with Joshua. As the pounding continued the steward's small figure emerged and shot to the door, muttering loudly.

"*Carámba! Qué hombre! Un momento.*"

The door banged open. "The señora is sleeping," he announced with dignity.

"She ain't either, she's standin' right behind you!"

"Manolo," I scolded angrily, "you had no business letting me sleep. You know I was supposed to relieve Mr. Hare for the second dog watch!"

"That ain't what I come about. It's somethin' more serious."

"Please come in, Mr. Hare." I lit several lamps as Manolo went for coffee. "Won't you have a seat?"

"No, ma'am. I'll stand. I got wind o' what you were talkin' about earlier today, and it's nearly broached me too."

My heart sank.

"It's Mr. Keeler, ma'am. No-good, double-tongued sea lawyer! He ain't fit to carry as ballast."

"I don't understand. What harm can he do locked away in the brig?"

"Plenty. He sneaked a letter to the deckhouse. Told the crew that if the captain ain't already dead he soon would be. And that no female's got a hope in ___ of steerin' this clipper 'round the Horn."

"I see." I stood very still. "Is that all?"

"Just about, ma'am. He said even if by some miracle we did escape from here without pilin' up on the rocks or scrapin' an iceberg, you'd never get us up the Peru coast. . . . The fact is, ma'am, the lads are scared. They believe Keeler. If we don't do something, fast, we're goin' to have a mutiny on our hands."

I sank down onto the sofa. I knew the second mate did not exaggerate. I also knew how quickly fear and anger could ignite into violence. . . . The scene in Hong Kong harbor replayed itself in my mind, and I saw the flash of sun on the barrel of Joshua's raised revolver. . . . Dear God! Now the master of the *Neptune's Car* lay in the next room, unable even to lift his head.

"I know how you feel about that Judas, Miz Patten. Myself, I'd rather take orders from Lucifer. But maybe there ain't no choice."

"*No!*" Anger spurted through me. "We *cannot* let that man take control of this ship. Especially now! Muster the crew, Mr. Hare. I want to talk to them."

The mate ran a hand through his beard. "Don't know as that's a good idea, Miz Patten. They're not feelin' too disposed to listen to you right now."

"As you pointed out, we haven't much choice." I added, more quietly, "I have to try at least, Mr. Hare. Please."

"Very good, ma'am. I'll have the lads by the lee lifeboat davits in five minutes. There's enough shelter there, they should be able to hear you."

"Mr. Hare?"

He turned back, his hand on the door.

"If there's trouble, if—if the men have already made up their minds against me—I won't expect you to take my part. It would be madness. And you have done enough—more than most men would do."

"Only done my duty as I seen it, ma'am. If Jonathan Hare can't stand by a lady like yourself when she's in trouble, then he's no man."

Left to myself, I began to pace. I should have anticipated something like this. Keeler's readiness to turn the crew's fear and superstition to his own advantage proved what kind of man he was. He must not be allowed to have his way! What was I to say to the crew, to convince them?

I stopped beside Joshua's bed. If only some miracle would happen, *now*, and those grey-blue eyes would focus on me and he would tell me what to do! I tried to pray, but it was meaningless.

"God is too far off," I whispered. "You always had the answers, Joshua. Why won't you help me?"

Suddenly Joshua's words flashed across my memory: "*I don't pretend to know all the answers, but I accept the ones God has given us in his book. . . . Maybe sometime you'll read them for yourself.*"

His book. I went to the shelf and took it down. It hurt just to hold it in my hands, it was so much a part of Joshua. How many hours had I watched him reading, absorbed, looking up to share something he thought significant? And how many times had I only pretended to listen?

I opened the book and absently leafed through the pages. Some of the verses had been underlined. Had they held a special message for him? Would they for me, too? I read the next verse I came to. A chill ran down my spine.

When thou passest through the waters, I will be with thee. . . .

It was as though, in that moment, Joshua had found some way of communicating with me. *Or was it not Joshua, but Joshua's God?*

The possibility overwhelmed me. I could not, did not want to dismiss it. With all my heart I wanted to believe that God cared for *me* that much. If he did I could face those men. I could face anything, if only I wasn't alone.

"*Dear God, be with me!*"

I whispered the words even as I drew on my cloak and bonnet and bent to brush my lips across Joshua's cheek. Then I picked up the lantern and started for the companionway steps.

I was glad for the lantern. The night was pitch black although it was not quite eight o'clock. I stood for a moment, steadying myself against the afterhouse, adjusting to the piercing cold and rolling deck; then forced myself forward. At least the wind had fallen. I would not even have to use the horn to be heard.

The men were a shadowy cluster under the lifeboat. I secured the lantern so that the light was upon me, and faced them. The mutter of their voices died away. I knew they were observing me, and that I must not betray the slightest trace of uncertainty or fear, or my cause would be lost. At the edge of my vision I saw Mr. Hare. He was leaning against the rail, a hand casually resting on the handle of a belaying pin. He nodded and touched his cap. My only friend? I thought it probable. Though the crew did not hate me personally, they were hostile toward the authority I represented. It was not for me or any of my sex to have such authority. It was against every tradition and superstition that had been bred into them.

I gripped the rail that separated me from the lower deck and in a loud, clear voice, began to speak. Most of the men knew only fragments of English, a kind of sailor's jargon that could be used on any merchant vessel. It was important to make myself understood.

"You have heard plenty of scuttlebut! You have also been told lies. I have called you together tonight so that you may hear the truth.

"As you know, Captain Patten was taken ill several days ago. He is not dead—nor is he dying. He will take over the command again. Until he does, I intend to carry on.

"Mr. Keeler would have you believe no woman is able to steer a ship. Some of you know that is not true. You have heard of Mrs. Cressy. For years she has navigated the clipper

Flying Cloud! And you have all seen me take the sights for Captain Patten many times. *He* believed I could do it, and I can.

"The *Neptune's Car* is a brave ship. She has a brave captain. I believe she also has a brave crew. I have seen each of you endure great suffering in the weeks already past. That is why I come to you and ask your help now for the days ahead. I cannot sail the *Neptune's Car* without you. But with your willing hands and hearts, and the grace of God, I have every confidence that we shall bring this ship safely into port!"

It was done. I had nothing more to say. The men below me were silent. Had I failed, then? I could not bear to face their mute faces any longer. I turned dully toward the companion-way. Then I heard my name.

"Mistress Patten!" It was the Swede, Lundquist. I swung around and saw him pulling off his jersey cap.

"You watch the helm, *ja?* We sail the ship!" His head swiveled menacingly. "Any Jack does not like it, he will say so now, to my face."

Nobody let out a sound.

"No? Is good!" he roared, and several joined in with a cheer. I didn't know whether to laugh or cry, the relief was so intense.

"All right then. That'll be all. Go below the watch!" Mr. Hare got the men moving again, and then joined me aft.

"Looks like you got Keeler scuppered, ma'am. The lads'd take this ship into hell if you asked 'em!"

"I sincerely hope, Mr. Hare, that isn't what I've done."

Back at my desk I faced the reality of carrying out my fine words. Triumph was quickly eroded by doubt. Then I thrust it deliberately aside. The time of decision past; and the choice was made.

Now we had only to face Cape Horn.

chapter 20

"Manolo."

"Sí, señora?"

I looked up from the medical guide I was reading and rubbed my eyes. Tiny lines of print continued to dance across my eyelids in a mocking reprise.

"Listen to this: *It is important to reduce all fevers. In the case of a long-continuing fever with delirium it is not an uncommon practice to shave the patient's head.* What do you think? Should we try it?"

The steward shrugged. "I do not know, señora. If that is what the book says. I will go and find the scissors."

"Wait. There's a pair here in my sewing basket." I fumbled for them.

He said, gently, "You like me to help, señora?"

I shook my head. "No. It's all right. He will be quieter if I do it."

I sat beside Joshua. For a moment my hands strayed through the fair hair that had grown so shaggy over the last weeks. Then, ruthlessly, I took the scissors and began to plow ragged furrows over his skull. A tear splashed on my hand, then another. I wiped them away angrily. Crying would not help Joshua, I told myself. Still, the tears came, and when I had finished my task I bowed my head on his chest, and wept unrestrainedly.

Joshua was getting weaker every day. None of the remedies or medications suggested in the books had done any good whatsoever. I had been forced to realize that whatever Joshua's ailment was, it was beyond my powers to diagnose—perhaps, even, to treat. But I must continue to try.

A glance at the barometer sent me topside. The wind was blowing hard from the northeast and rain was just beginning to slice from the heavens. Men aloft were taking in sail.

"The glass is falling fast!" I shouted to the mate. He nodded. "Hold on to all the canvas you can!"

The bowsprit dived into a huge crest, burying the unfortunate sailors in water up to their necks, then pitching them into the air.

The lookout shouted suddenly from the mizzen mast. "*Distress flairs! Port quarter!*" I called for the telescope, but couldn't make anything out through the mist.

"Shall we send up an answering flair?"

"I wouldn't advise it, ma'am."

"But there's a ship out there in distress!"

"Aye, and so are we, if it comes to that."

Another flare appeared, further astern.

"She must be heading for Rio."

"Miz Pattern, we ain't got any choice. There's less than an hour of daylight left and a storm brewin'. Even if we hunted that ship down in time, we could never work close to her in these seas without smashin' us both to kindlin'!"

I lowered the telescope. *If Joshua were here, giving the orders,* I thought, *we could do it.* But he wasn't here. The unknown ship would have to solve its problems without us.

The storm that roared down on us that black September night turned out to be the worst that we had yet encountered. For forty-eight hours there was no rest for anyone. I dared not leave the quarterdeck for more than a few minutes at a time, calculating our drift, shouting orders to the helm through a trumpet, sometimes lurching from the binnacle to shelter in the companionway for a cup of coffee. The cold passed gradually into numbness but my horror did not. Ton after ton of water cascaded onto the decks below in a welter of foam. Again and again, our gallant ship rose and shook it off. I marveled at her resilience. How long could she keep it up? Any attempt to set sail was futile; heavy canvas split apart like flimsy cotton cloth. We ran on, helpless before the gale.

Once, emerging from the companionway, I was caught by a towering wave breaking over the stern. With a shriek I felt myself slammed hard against the deck and pulled under. I thought, *this is the end. I'm going to die.* And then the water drained away, and I could breathe.

I pulled myself up, wet to the skin.

The baby. What about my baby?

For the first time in days I remembered the life inside me. Was he all right? He had to be—and *I* had to be. There was no time for anything else.

At daybreak on the third day, the winds slackened enough that I could order reefed topsails and fore courses. We braced the yards, and then began a hard beat to windward.

Perhaps it was just as well during those nightmarish weeks that there was so little chance for sleep. Days and nights blurred together under the unending necessity of working up our position and laying out a course, consulting with Mr. Hare, standing frozen vigils on the quarterdeck and deciding when to strike sail and when to set it. What sleep I stole was tormented with dreams of disaster and death. And always—overriding all else—was my anxiety for Joshua.

The crew had been magnificent. For eighteen days of misery off the Horn and another week of gales in the roaring forties, they had endured boils, crushed fingers, bruised ribs, darkness, cold and wet. They had carried on when others would have turned back. And now, at last, the worst was over.

On the twenty-fifth day of September I opened the log book and wrote: *Latitude 40°19', Longitude 78°48'. This day continued fresh breezes and clear sky. All sails set and drawing.*

Joshua would be proud, I thought. There was so much I longed to share with him. More than anything else, I wanted to tell him about our child. His son. Pain twisted inside me. I shut the log abruptly and stood up.

"Mary?"

It was Joshua's voice. I stood frozen, straining my ears, and then I heard it again. I ran into the next room and found him waiting, his eyes lucid and alert.

"Oh, Joshua!" The tears that I had held back so long streamed down my cheeks. I knelt beside his bed. "Have you really come back to me? I've missed you so much, my darling!"

Very slowly, he lifted one hand and touched my hair.

"How long?" he whispered.

"Three weeks. It seemed like years. Forever." I saw alarm in his eyes and added quickly, "We're all right, Joshua. We've doubled the Horn."

"But—Keeler—"

"Mr. Keeler is where you put him. In the brig."

"Then how—?"

"Don't try to talk any more," I put my fingers over his lips. "Rest, while I get you something to eat."

I left him to give Manolo orders for broth. When I returned, Joshua was already asleep, his fragile store of strength exhausted. I stood watching the normal rise and fall of his breathing. His skin felt quite cool to the touch. My heart filled with gratitude.

Several hours later, Joshua woke from a sound sleep and managed to down a good deal of the broth Manolo brought. Now he was impatient for answers.

"I still don't understand. How have you managed . . . all this time?"

"Well, I haven't been entirely alone, you know. There's Mr. Hare. He's been wonderful. And the third mate, Stefenack. And, of course, the crew. Joshua, they've worked so hard—" I broke off, chuckling.

"Don't look so cynical. It's true! You wouldn't recognize them from the lot you shipped in New York."

"Then you must have worked a miracle."

"You always did underestimate me, captain." I ran a finger along the too-prominent ridge of his cheekbone. "Not that there weren't a few bad moments along the way."

"About Keeler, Mary—"

"He was one of the bad moments. Or have you already guessed? He was certain he had to take over the quarterdeck or we'd all go to the bottom. Of course, I wouldn't let him. I said that was up to you. Imagine how furious he was when the crew supported me."

"You'll have to release him, Mary."

"*What?*" I stared at him blankly.

"I don't pretend to like the man. He's arrogant and he's done a sparyard job as first mate. But maybe he's learned his lesson. He knows how to navigate, Mary. He can take away some of the strain you're under."

"But we've already doubled Cape Horn! And passed the forties. The worst part is over."

He shook his head. "There's the rest of the Peru Current and thousands more sea miles between us and San Francisco. Anything could happen."

"But you're getting better now, Joshua! Mr. Hare can help me until you're able to take over again."

"I'm a long way from taking command again. Face it. You can't be expected to know how to deal with every problem that comes up."

"I've done pretty well so far."

"God helping you, yes. But you're tired. Don't you think I know what you've been through? How much longer do you think you can keep it up?"

The temptation to yield to him was powerful. What bliss it would be to shift the weight of responsibility to someone else!

"But Mr. Keeler—I just don't know, Joshua."

"You don't have to know. Trust my judgment. Let me make the decision." He waited until I nodded.

"Good." He sighed deeply and I stood up.

"That's enough talk for now."

"Mary. Promise me you'll give the order."

"I promise."

Softly I closed the door behind me and leaned against it. Then I went on deck to find Mr. Hare.

The order to release Keeler was about as popular as I expected it to be. The mate gaped at me thunderstruck.

"You sure, ma'am? You sure the cap'n ain't still out of his head?"

"I am, Mr. Hare."

"Well, it's good news the old man's better, ma'am, and that's a fact. But it don't seem right lettin' Keeler take over. Not after all we been through to muzzle him."

"Mr. Hare," I said a little sharply. "You have Captain Patten's instruction. You will please carry it out."

"Aye, ma'am."

"The captain would not order anything that wasn't for the good of the ship."

"No, ma'am."

While the mate passed the word I went to fetch the sextant from its case for the three o'clock reading. Returning, I paused to lift my face to the unaccustomed brightness of the sun.

"I'd almost forgotten how glorious it is to be alive, Mr. Hare. Sometimes I thought I'd never see the sun again."

"None of us ever guessed that, ma'am."

He was about to add something more when Mr. Keeler came up the steps.

"Time on your hands, mister? The sheets want trimming, in case you haven't noticed." He looked and sounded exactly as he always had.

The second mate said stiffly, "I'll be within call if you need me, ma'am."

As he strode forward I tried to conquer a sudden, unreasonable fear.

"And do you think you will be needing him, Mistress Patten?" The mate smiled.

"I am much indebted to Mr. Hare for his assistance."

"You were steering pretty close to the wind, with only yourself and a second greaser in charge. The men might have taken matters into their own hands."

"But they didn't, did they?"

"You were lucky." He shrugged, then looked me deliberately up and down. "If you want to go below I'll take care of things now."

"In point of fact, Mr. Keeler, I was about to take the

altitude. The captain may have reinstated you as first officer, but you cannot dismiss me from the quarterdeck as easily as you did Mr. Hare."

"So, it was the captain's idea. No need to get touchy with me. If you'd would rather stay topside that's just dandy. Couldn't be very much fun for someone like you nursing a sick man."

I made an effort to keep my voice under control. "I have no intention of shirking my responsibilities, either to my husband or the *Neptune's Car*. Be certain you feel the same way, Mr. Keeler. Just one sign of disobedience or carelessness and you'll find yourself back in the brig."

I took the reading and went below. The rest of the afternoon and evening stretched luxuriously before me. What should I do? Passing by a looking glass, I chanced to catch a reflection of myself, and paused. The girl who stared back at me was a pale-faced, hollow-eyed stranger. Dark hair straggled down untidily to my shoulders. *I look almost twice my age!* I thought, appalled.

Manolo was dispatched for a quantity of hot water. Repairing the damages would not be an easy task. My skin had been roughened by exposure to salt water and could not bear scrubbing. I soaked for a long time and then stepped, shivering, from the tin bath, smoothing myself all over with fragrant oil. Then I slipped on a fresh cotton shift and brushed my hair until it crackled with vitality. How marvelous to feel clean again! Perhaps, after a full night's sleep, I would be more like my old self.

Hearing Joshua's voice in the next room I tiptoed to the door and peeked in.

"Did you call, captain?"

"I thought I heard you moving around." His eyes brightened as they traveled over me. "Maybe you'd better get in here beside me before you catch a chill."

"Excellent idea, captain, sir." I snuggled obediently under the blankets and was rewarded by a long and thorough kiss.

"Mm. . . . I've waited a long time for that!"

"Poor little girl." His fingers traced the circles under my eyes. "It will be over soon, my love. You'll only remember this as a bad dream."

"It hasn't been all bad, Joshua. I've learned an awful lot. And—oh, there's so much to tell you!"

"Shh. First tell me that you've done as I asked about Keeler."

"Yes." I nodded. "He's been released."

"Good. Now I want you to rest. You're worn out."

"*Now?* But I can't. I haven't been on deck since three. I ought to just—"

"Don't be insubordinate, woman, or I'll have you tied to this berth."

"Ah, captain, you're a hard man to argue with! I suppose . . . just for an hour or two . . . it wouldn't do any harm." I closed my eyes. After a minute I opened them again.

"Are you just going to lie there staring at me?"

"I am. Now be quiet."

I sighed happily. It wouldn't do, of course, to stay here long. It was necessary to keep an eye on Mr. Keeler and see how the men were getting on with him. And I must be certain we were carrying all the sail we possibly could. . . . My brain wearily ticked off my list of duties. And then it betrayed me by plunging me into forgetfulness.

chapter
21

I slept very late the next morning. When I woke I felt refreshed, as I had not for many weeks.

Joshua's blue gaze was already upon me.

"Good heavens, you haven't been awake all night, have you? Look at the time. You should have gotten me up!"

I rolled out of bed. Still clad in only my thin shift, I poured water into the basin and splashed it onto my face.

"Are you hungry? Perhaps I can get Doc to make you a proper omelet."

"Mary."

"Mm?" I blotted my face with a towel. When he didn't answer I went to stand beside him. "Aren't you feeling well this morning? You look—peculiar."

"Why didn't you tell me?"

"Tell you what, Joshua?"

"Did you think you could hide it from me? I know your body as well as my own."

My hands flew involuntarily to my stomach. "I guess I've gained a little weight."

"In the name of heaven, Mary! Why did you want to keep it from me?"

"I didn't! I didn't want to! But you were so worried about the ship and getting around the Horn. I didn't think it was the right time. And then you got sick, and it was too late—" I covered my face with my hands. "You can't know how it's been, waiting and hoping, every day—"

"My darling. I'm so sorry," he whispered.

"You're not sorry about the baby?" I took my hands from my eyes. "You do want him, don't you?"

"Of course I do! It's what I've prayed for."

"Oh, Joshua," I dropped down beside him, "I think I'm the happiest and proudest woman on the seven seas. It's going to be a boy, of course. A namesake for you!"

He pressed my fingers to his lips. "A girl would be fine, too. So long as she isn't contrary like her mother."

"Better contrary than pig-headed! But you have to have a son first. Then a daughter. After that we'll have a half dozen more, assorted."

We laughed, raptly contemplating the future.

"When do you figure he's due?"

"March, I think. About six months."

"You'll have to be more careful from now on. Build up your strength."

"Speaking of building strength, it's high time I fixed you some breakfast." I got up and finished dressing, pleasurably aware of his eyes upon me.

He muttered, "You're as thin as a mizzen mast."

"Am I? Better enjoy it. I'll soon be so fat I'll waddle."

When I opened the door he stopped me. "I love you, Mary. Very, very much. Don't ever forget that."

I went out, my heart singing.

A short while later I emerged onto the deck. Mr. Keeler

was standing near the binnacle. He observed my appearance with raised eyebrows and a knowing smile.

"Well, well. You're in fine trim this morning."

"Why not? A mood to match the weather. Don't you think it's time to fly those skysails, Mr. Keeler?"

"No, ma'am. I don't."

"Perhaps we ought to ask Mr. Hare's opinion," I replied coolly, and his smile flickered out.

"There's only one first officer aboard this ship. Until the captain's fit to take the quarterdeck I don't share it with anyone."

I knew he was right, nor would Joshua approve of my tampering with the chain of command.

"Very well, Mr. Keeler. As you think best."

I remained on deck until high noon. After the sights were taken I proposed that we both retire and work up our position. We could then compare notes in an hour.

Returning to the cabin I set to work at once. It was amazing, I thought, what a night's sleep could do. All of the strain of the previous weeks seemed to have disappeared. Joshua was right. Whether I liked Mr. Keeler or not, the burden was lighter.

After a short period with pencil and paper, however, I studied my figures with puzzlement. The longitude was off; there had to be an error in the arithmetic somewhere. Frowning, I took up my pencil and carefully went through the formula once more.

The result was identical: *latitude 30°47', longitude 76°09'.* The *Neptune's Car* was veering to the northeast. I pinpointed our position on the chart and with growing dismay saw we were headed directly toward the Chilean port of Valparaiso.

Refusing to wait for the appointed time, I raced across the saloon and hammered on the door of the mate's quarters.

"Mr. Keeler, I demand that you open this door!"

It opened abruptly, catching me off guard. I literally fell against the mate. His arms came around me at once, and when I pulled away he laughed, a soft, intimate laugh.

"You wanted something special, ma'am?"

"Yes. I do," I said, struggling to regain my composure. "You can explain to me why this ship is off course!"

He shrugged. "Afraid I don't know what you're talking about."

"No? You must think me very stupid, sir. Or did you really think you could make port before anyone realized what you were up to?"

"It sounds to me, ma'am, like you made a mistake in your reckoning. Why don't you check it over?"

"There is no mistake, Mr. Keeler."

His dark eyes were unfathomable. "I assume you've already reported this to the captain?"

"No. I have no wish to upset Captain Patten unless it is absolutely necessary. I am willing to give you the benefit of the doubt, Mr. Keeler. Correct our heading—*now*, and the matter will go no further."

He folded his arms and lounged against the doorframe. "That's real nice of you, Mistress Patten, ma'am. But as far as I'm concerned we're right on course. I can't go against common sense, can I? Not even to please you."

Furious, I turned my back and hurried back through the saloon to the cabin. Joshua was awake. When he saw my face he demanded, "What happened?"

"It's Keeler. I knew we could never trust that man! It was a mistake to release him."

"Calm down and tell me. Is he shortening sail again?"

"I wish that were all." I took a deep breath. "Joshua, Keeler's altered our course. He's steering for Valparaiso."

"Val—? Are you sure?"

"Positive. He denies it, of course. Claims my reckoning is off."

"Did you ask for his results?"

"No. What good would that do? He'd only have come up with a false position."

Joshua lifted a hand to cover his eyes as if they pained him.

"If only I could. . . . Mary, bring me your figures. Let me go over them."

I asked, slowly, "Is that what you think, Joshua? That I've made a mistake?"

"I don't know what to think. What would Keeler gain by taking us into port? He knows I'd have him arrested for mutiny the minute we touched anchor."

Silently I went to fetch the worksheet. For several minutes Joshua held it with trembling hands before sinking back wearily.

"It's no use. My eyes. They keep blurring."

"Then there's no way to convince you. It's just my word against his." I bit my lip. "What if Mr. Hare verified my opinion?"

"He and Keeler have always been at loggerheads. He'd likely swear to anything to send the mate back to the brig. No, I'll have a word with Keeler. Ask him to report to me, Mary."

This time I would not make the mistake of going myself. The steward delivered Joshua's order and the mate presented himself promptly, neatly groomed and respectful in manner. *The image of the model officer,* I thought, disgusted.

"You sent for me, captain?"

"I did. Mrs. Patten has brought a serious charge against you. She believes you are deliberately disobeying orders and making for Valparaiso, Mr. Keeler."

"I'd be the last to speak ill against Mistress Patten, sir. She's earned the respect of the whole crew. But it's easy to make a mistake when you've been under the kind of strain she's been under."

"Then you insist we are holding our original course?"

The mate's eyes shifted to me. He had no way of knowing whether or not Joshua had verified my calculations. To insist we were on course if Joshua had already proven otherwise would seal his fate.

"Aye, sir. We are tacking against strong headwinds, of course. You know yourself we can't always bear due north in the Peru Current. But Frisco's where we're bound."

For an endless moment Joshua's blue eyes burned into Keeler as if he were trying to penetrate his thoughts. Finally he nodded.

"Very well, mister. Return to your duties. But remember this: I am still master of this vessel. Confined to a berth or not, I intend to see that my orders are carried out."

"Aye, aye, sir." The mate allowed the shadow of a smile. "No chance I'll forget that, sir." Without sparing another glance at me he left the cabin. I looked after him, horrified.

"You aren't going to let him have his way? He's lying! Can't you see that?"

Joshua struggled to sit up. "I need your help, Mary. Set up a cot near the compass so I can watch it. If Keeler's lying we'll soon find out."

"But you shouldn't—"

"Do as I say. Please."

Against all my instincts, I obeyed. Joshua's face was ashen as he half-staggered, half-fell onto the hastily set-up cot. He lay there gasping for so long I cried out, "Nothing is worth this! Joshua, let the man do what he wants. Maybe Valparaiso isn't such a terrible idea. There would be a doctor there, medicine—"

"*No.*"

What would he do, I wondered, *if the situation was reversed, and I was the one who was ill?* His contract with the shipowners specified that under no circumstances was the ship to be taken into any other port than San Francisco. Was honor more important to Joshua than his life?

I poured a glass of water and held it to his lips. Every ounce of strength he had left was concentrated on the compass. As seconds ticked agonizingly into minutes I moved about restlessly, straightening the cabin, and then went to stare out of the porthole at the sea. Always, always, the same watery panorama. What wouldn't I give for the sight of land and houses and green, growing things?

"I'm going on deck for some air," I said abruptly. "You don't mind?"

He moved his head slightly. "No . . . go ahead."

I pulled a wrap over my shoulders and hurried up the steps. The wind snatched at me as I stepped onto the deck, but I was glad for it. I walked aft to the taffrail, fixing my eyes on the white ribbon of our wake.

"Old Man didn't listen to you, did he?"

I stiffened, and replied without turning.

"You will soon find out, Mr. Keeler, that the captain isn't easy to deceive. He is still very much in control of this ship."

"Is he now?" he answered. "The man I just saw in your cabin couldn't skipper a rowboat. No more than he can husband you."

I spun around, my hand upraised to strike him, but he caught my wrist.

"You—how dare you?"

"I dare a lot of things, if they're important enough."

"Like slowing us up and steering us off course?"

"Could be."

"But *why?*"

"You've got a head on your shoulders. I'll let you figure it out."

I tried to walk away but he stepped closer, pinning me against the rail.

"Let me pass."

"I don't know as I will. I don't think you really want me to."

He reached out to gather a fistful of the hair that had fallen loose across my shoulders. "You're a handsome woman, Mary. I've always thought so."

"I can scream," I whispered, terror gripping my throat.

"Aye, you can. And when the crew comes running I'll have to explain how the poor mistress got took with a dizzy spell and fell overboard."

"You wouldn't!"

He laughed, releasing my hair. I seized the opportunity to slip sidewise and ran for the companionway.

Why didn't I shout, then, for the helmsman or someone else who might have heard me? There was no rhyme or logic in what I did—only blind, unreasoning panic. I stumbled, heard the sound of boots in pursuit, and fled down the narrow companionway steps with my breath coming in ragged sobs.

At the bottom I burst through the cabin door and turned to shoot the bolt. The door was kicked out of my hands, and then the mate stood there, smiling hideously.

"Joshua—somebody—*help me, please!*"

I was aware, vaguely, of Joshua on the cot in back of me trying to rise, but I could not take my eyes from Keeler's face. He took a step closer.

Suddenly the gloating triumph—the utter assurance that nothing could stop him—filled me with rage. I backed against the desk and groped behind me for a weapon. My hand closed over a brass paperweight.

"I'm warning you! Don't come any closer!"

Deliberately, tauntingly, he took another step. I picked up the weight and hurled it with all my strength. It grazed Keeler's head, and he stopped short, a stunned expression in his eyes. Then he crashed heavily to the deck.

"Mrs. Patten, ma'am, you all right?"

Mr. Hare and a half dozen others of the crew, armed with belaying pins and handspikes, swarmed into the cabin.

"I'm—afraid there's been a dreadful accident, Mr. Hare."

One of the men swore. "If that limb of Satan's laid one finger on you—"

"*Mary.*"

I turned slowly in the direction of Joshua's voice. His face was a mask of pain.

"I'm all right. Truly." I would have gone to him, but my legs suddenly refused to support me. I sat down. My eyes fastened with a dreadful fascination on the man who sprawled a few feet away with blood trickling from his scalp.

"Mister Hare?"

"Aye, captain!"

"You and these men stand as witnesses. Mr. Keeler is from this moment relieved of all further duty aboard the *Neptune's Car*."

"Aye, aye, sir!"

"You, Mr. Hare, will hereafter serve as first officer." He paused, forcing himself on with an effort. "You will appoint a second mate and assist Mrs. Patten in every way possible. Let it be known to the crew that we will make no port but San Francisco. Is that understood?"

"Understood, captain. Will that be all?"

Joshua closed his eyes. For a moment I thought he was done speaking, but when his eyes opened again they were blazing with anger.

"Just get that animal out of my sight! Tell him if he makes one more false move—even in the brig—I will cheerfully see him strung from the yards!"

The crew slung the mate over their shoulders and dragged him out roughly through the saloon. Mr. Hare threw me a concerned look and then followed.

"You were right," Joshua said hoarsely. "I was a fool to allow Keeler his freedom."

"Hush. Don't talk now."

"I couldn't even take your word for it that we were off course! I had more faith in the instruments."

"You did what you thought was right."

"I've failed, Mary. As a captain and as your husband."

"No! Don't say that!"

"Can you know how it felt, lying here helpless while that brute came after you?"

His voice broke. Beads of sweat stood on his forehead and I pleaded, "Stop torturing yourself. Please, Joshua! It's all over."

His eyelids fluttered shut. I bent forward, frightened, to watch the shallow rise and fall of his chest. How long I stayed in that position I do not know.

"Señora?"

The steward appeared in the doorway. His round face was troubled. "I stay with the captain, señora. Maybe you go and rest now, sí?"

"Lie down? No, no, I can't do that. There's the course. I have to see about changing our course."

I rose from my crouched position. The cabin tilted oddly, then righted itself.

"Do not worry about the captain, señora. Mañana, he will be better. You will see."

"Yes."

Tomorrow, he said. Perhaps Joshua would wake and be able to forget what had happened today. But how could I? The weight of responsibility that had lifted so briefly from my shoulders settled down again, more heavily than ever. I went to give the helmsman his orders.

When I slept that night I dreamed that I was running through endless corridors and echoing rooms, trying to escape some unimaginable horror. No matter how fast I ran I could hear the dreadful progress of the thing behind me. And then, suddenly, I tripped and fell. With a shriek of triumph my pursuer was upon me, tall and menacing. Then it brought its face close.

It was the face of death.

"*Joshua!*"

I sat up, still shaking from the vividness of the dream, wide-eyed with fear. "Joshua?" I reached over to touch him.

It was then that the realization broke over me: it was not I but Joshua who was in danger. The blazing skin told me that the fever had returned, dragging him away from me again into unconsciousness.

chapter
22

Men at sea have a particular dread of fire. They know that if the flames are not put out at once there will be little they can do to keep their ship—and themselves—from total destruction.

It was with the same sort of helplessness that I watched the fires spreading out of control within Joshua. There were days when Manolo and I were forced to bind him with strips of cloth so that he could not throw himself from the berth. Other times the fever burned so low that we would begin to look again for a recovery.

The *Neptune's Car* pressed north. Flaunting her fine weather suit of lighter sails, she scarcely even needed a yard braced. I grew impatient with speeds of twelve and thirteen knots and ordered the studding booms run out.

"You're a driver, sure enough," grinned Mr. Hare approvingly. "Gettin' more like the Old Man every day."

I winced. There was a vast sea of difference between my decisions and Joshua's. His were based on knowledge and experience, mine were most often a guess. I lost count of how many times I laid too much stress on the clipper's top hamper and sacrificed sails to the wind. Once, after men were sent aloft with palms and needles to keep a foresail tear from spreading, the canvas blew out completely. A wildly flailing rope knocked one of the men unconscious, and I felt responsible.

For the most part, however, the crew's duties aloft were not strenuous. As I watched them mend the damages of the Horn, an indigo sky overhead and the wind singing in the sails, I thought how content I would be, if only Joshua stood well and strong at my side.

But with each passing day that likelihood seemed more remote. The books could offer no help. The medicines had almost run out. I found myself turning more often to another book, the one I thought of as Joshua's.

I told myself that it was only sentiment that drew me to the Bible, but it was more than that. The message of the words fascinated me. After browsing through scattered verses I began reading through the whole Gospel of St. John. It amazed me that in all the years of attending church I had never done so before. No wonder Jesus had always been a shadowy figure to me. For the first time I saw him as a real person, deity who had chosen to take human form.

But why would God want to do that? It seemed incredible that he should not be born, at least, as a king instead of a carpenter's son. And why would he allow men to take his life from him?

The character of Jesus was intriguing. I had the oddest feeling that I was seeing glimpses of Joshua in him. Then it dawned that it was the other way around. I had seen the person of Jesus in Joshua. The conclusion stunned me. What was it Joshua had told me that day on the hill? *You say there's a part of me you can't seem to get close to. . . . He's that part, Mary.*

I looked for answers and found them. *I am come in my Father's name. . . . I am come that they might have life, and that they might have it more abundantly. . . . To this end was I born, and for this cause came I into the world, that I should bear witness to the truth. . . . For God so loved the world, that he gave his only begotten Son, that whosoever believeth in him should not perish, but have everlasting life.*

At the close of the book the apostle John declared his reason for writing: *But these are written that ye might believe that Jesus is the Christ, the Son of God; and that believing ye might have life through his name.*

Life. Abundant life. Everlasting life. Was it possible that Jesus could set me forever free from my fear of death? Could God really have loved me enough to allow his son to take my hell—so that I could experience his heaven?

Tears coursed down my face. I believed that was what he had done.

"No wonder Joshua loves you!" I whispered. Why had it taken me so long to see it? "You waited, just as Joshua waited, for me to come to the end of myself, nineteen years. Thank you for not giving up on me."

I felt a peculiar lightness. It was similar to the relief I had at first experienced when Mr. Keeler briefly took over the quarterdeck, and it puzzled me until I recognized why. I was no longer alone. Outward circumstances remained unchanged, but the ultimate responsibility for them had been given into another's hands.

My Captain was at the helm.

Joshua continued to drift in and out of consciousness. Sometimes he was well enough to take a small amount of solid food, or respond when I spoke to him. But this was rare. Most days, even when he was conscious, he seemed not to understand what was going on. I worried at the effect the prolonged fever was having.

One evening as I sat by the bed, doing some mending, he suddenly demanded in a trembling voice to know who was in the cabin with him.

"It's only me, Joshua, sewing."

"Mary? Why . . . why is it so dark?"

"It's past midnight. Would you like me to turn up the lamp?"

"Shadows. Everything is . . . shadows," he murmured as I unhooked the lantern and brought it close.

"There, that's better, isn't it?"

He stared at me. A shiver ran down my spine.

"Joshua? *Isn't it?*"

"You . . . are so beautiful."

I laughed, my relief was so intense. "You're impossible! Don't frighten me like that!" When he did not respond I asked, "How about if I read to you awhile?" I picked up the Bible but he had already closed his eyes. Later, then, I thought. But later didn't come.

I was on the quarterdeck the next afternoon when Manolo rushed up to me.

"The captain, señora! I think something is wrong. I talk to him and he looks right at me and acts like he does not know who I am. He will not answer me."

"It's all right, Manolo. Maybe he needs to tell me something."

I could hear Joshua shouting my name as I hurried down the steps and through the outer cabin. I stopped at the threshold and saw that his face was turned toward me. The blue eyes were full of torment.

"I'm here, my love. What is it? Would you like some water?"

I moved over to the bureau and poured a glass from the pitcher. Joshua didn't take his eyes from the doorway.

"Why don't they come?" he whispered restlessly. "I keep calling but nobody comes to light the lamp."

"*Joshua! Look at me!*"

I walked nearer to the bed. Then, deliberately, I let the glass slip from my hand. It shattered to the deck in a thousand pieces. Joshua didn't blink.

"Dear God, no! Please! *Don't let this happen to him!*"

But it had already happened, I realized. The disease that had robbed Joshua of his strength had now paralyzed his sight and hearing.

Grief flooded over me. I sank to the deck beside my husband and wept.

The southeast trades carried us along almost three days after we crossed the line between North and South Pacific. Then the wind let go, and we wallowed in the doldrums.

It was, perhaps, the most difficult part of the voyage to that point. Rounding the Horn, fighting through the roaring forties, I had drawn strength from the sheer business of survival. Now time hung heavily. The heat of the cabin made me uncomfortable and dizzy. I watched Joshua slip deeper into unconsciousness, and tried not to remember that it was at this latitude, on the last voyage, that Sinbad had died.

At night, after the blazing sun had dipped below the horizon, I took to pacing the decks. I prayed for many things during those hours: for a wind, for Joshua's life, for the life of our child. I told God that I would never ask for anything more if only Joshua could see his son. I walked until I was too exhausted to take another step. Then I stumbled below to await the dawn.

On the fourth day, a breeze sprang up. The canvas was unfurled and the *Neptune's Car* spread her wings. The last stretch! I listened to the chanties ringing out and felt renewed hope. We would make it after all. All of us.

"Never seen a crew so willin' to work, without standin' over 'em with a marlin spike!" observed Mr. Hare, a smile playing around his lips.

"They're anxious to make port. Who can blame them?"

"It's more than that, ma'am. The lads have sworn to polish this clipper till she looks like she just come off the ways. When the *Neptune's Car* opens the Golden Gate she'll hold her head high, ladylike and Bristol fashion! For your sake, ma'am."

"Mine?"

"Aye. Ain't no secret what the men think of you."

There was a constriction in my throat. "No more than I think of them, Mr. Hare."

November 3. Latitude 35° 44', Longitude 131° 13'. Strong Northwest winds, rain squally.

I put down the pen and stared at the entry. Only another five hundred miles, I thought. Two days and nights, and we should be off the Heads.

I went into Joshua's cabin. I had formed the habit lately of talking and reading to him as though he could hear. As I bent over him now, grieving over the thinness of his face, the transparency of his skin, I murmured, "It's almost over, my darling. God has kept you alive. Soon he'll make you well."

With the end so near I was filled with nervous exhilaration. I was torn between spending my time on deck, urging the ship to greater speeds, and staying with Joshua. The mates clearly preferred me below. Each time I lifted my eyes to the top hamper they braced themselves for an order to shake out more sail. They were not often disappointed.

On the second night I slept, exhausted, and woke to unearthly silence. When I ran on deck I discovered the wind had vanished. Thick, grey layers of fog were wound about our ship in an impossible-to-penetrate cocoon. Our flight had been suspended.

It was the final frustration of the whole heart-breaking journey. Two days, five, then a whole week passed. Still we drifted, with no sign of the fog lifting. By the tenth day, my taut nerves were stretched to the breaking point.

"Why, God?" I cried, on my knees. "Why has this happened? Why *now?* I've tried so hard, Father, but I just can't do any more. I'm tired. It's up to you now. Do what you think best."

I got up and laid down on the berth beside Joshua. The ship rose and fell beneath me, and I thought back to the first time I had lain here, wondering how I would ever be able to call the *Neptune's Car* my home. Now every motion, every creak of timber was as familiar to me as if I'd been born to it.

Suddenly my body stiffened. That sound. Was it—? I strained to listen, unbelieving, then heard it again. In an instant I was on my feet, wrapping a cloak around my shoulders and dashing up the companionway steps onto the quarterdeck. The light was just breaking through the mist. I lifted my eyes. Nothing was yet visible, but there was no doubt. The ruffle of heavy canvas, the slap of rope against spar could mean only one thing. *Wind.*

Mr. Hare came up beside me. I could see his homely, bearded face reflecting the same jubilation that was on mine.

"Fog's beginning' to break up already, ma'am. Another hour and the *Car*'ll be liftin' her skirts and dancin' into Frisco!"

"To God be the glory, Mr. Hare! Call all hands about ship. Prepare to brace up the after yards and swing the spanker around. Lively, now!"

Shortly before noon on the fifteenth day of November, we sighted the Farallon Islands. The mate squinted through the telescope and grunted unhappily.

"Not a single pilot boat in sight, ma'am. We'll have to lay off and wait till someone's available."

"*Wait?* We haven't come this far to sit and cool our heels, Mr. Hare!"

"There's a sandbar linin' that channel ahead. Steer too close to Point Bonita and the rip could spin us halfway around."

"I know the hazards, Mr. Hare." I studied him, holding my head to one side. "You've trusted me all this way, can't you trust just a little way longer?"

He hesitated. Then he nodded, slowly. "Aye, ma'am. Reckon I can."

"*Good.* Brace the yards and give us just enough sail to keep us moving. I'll take the wheel."

Perhaps it was a mad, reckless thing to do. Perhaps, under the circumstances, there was nothing else I could do. I only know I felt a perfect calm as I stood at the helm with the great ship under my hands. The men jumped onto the ropes and furled sail with a will. Then I pointed the *Neptune's Car* straight for the Golden Gate.

> I thought I heard the skipper say,
> Leave her, Johnnie, leave her!
> We'll go ashore and get our pay.
> It's time for us to leave her!

The clipper nosed past Signal Hill and opened the bay, and a boisterous cheer broke from the throats of the crew. Before us lay a fleet of anchored ships. In a few minutes we were among them, our cable splashing down for the first time in that long, arduous voyage.

"Miz Patten, ma'am?" The mate cleared his throat. On his face was a look of profound admiration. "I guess I owe you an apology."

"Mr. Hare," I smiled. "You don't owe me a thing."

A boat was lowered. Manolo rowed off with orders to fetch

a doctor while the rest of the crew raced through their duties. A flotilla of boarding house runners surrounded us, crying allurements. By the time the agent and consignee came aboard, my earlier exhilaration was gone. I felt only unutterably weary.

"One hundred thirty-six days, gentlemen," I said as I turned over the manifest. "Not very good time, I'm afraid."

"I'd say your time was outstanding, considering the odds! And I've never seen a ship in better trim. The owners owe you a great deal, Mrs. Patten. I am certain they will wish to express their commendation personally."

The doctor was a kindly, dignified-looking German named Welcker. After examining Joshua he suggested we move to a hotel without delay.

"I think you would both be more comfortable. The dampness and fog of the waterfront could be harmful, you see."

I nodded. "Whatever you think best."

"I shall make the arrangements. Would you prefer any particular accommodation, madam?"

"I don't know, I—" I passed a hand over my eyes. "The Oriental Hotel perhaps. Joshua and I stayed there before."

"Excellent."

He went off, promising to attend his patient at the hotel in a short while. I gathered together some clothing and a few personal items. More than that would be like admitting the possibility that we weren't going to return. I was grateful when Mr. Hare insisted on escorting us from the ship.

The Oriental was even grander than I remembered. Elegantly dressed ladies and gentlemen stared curiously as we entered the lobby with Joshua's litter, borne by two husky seamen, and trooped up the steps. I gripped the mate's arm, glad for the concealment of my cloak.

"I never even thought to change my dress," I whispered. "Isn't that odd. Appearance used to be so important to me."

Mr. Hare excused himself almost at once to return to the ship. I unpacked a few things, then sat down by Joshua to await the doctor. He was not long in coming.

"My dear Mistress Patten, what is this? I give you time to avail yourself of a hot meal and bath, and you have not stirred from this chair!"

"Doctor, my husband's survival has been the concern of every waking moment for the past two months. Can you blame me for not being able to relax? I must know, sir. Can you give him back to me?"

"Only God has the power over life and death, Mrs. Patten. I can promise only to do my best. My experience with cases of brain fever is limited."

"Brain fever. That's what it is, then?"

It would seem so from all that you have told me. It is when a congestion settles in the brain that the patient loses certain of his senses. But the blindness and deafness are only symptoms of the disease. The disease must be controlled before the sight and hearing can return."

He folded his stethoscope. "I would like to suggest someone to help with the nursing."

"That won't be necessary. I am prepared to care for my husband."

"I don't question your willingness, Mistress Patten. I am convinced your devotion has kept the captain alive. However, in your condition—"

"I am quite fit, I assure you. Besides, it's too late to start pampering me, I wouldn't know what to do with myself."

He sighed. "Very well, we shall see how things go. But I will insist that you take proper rest and nourishment."

No one had to urge me that night. After a meal which

reminded me of all I had missed, I soaked in the bathtub and then climbed into a massive featherbed. Oblivion enveloped me. Twelve o'clock, four o'clock, eight, for the first time in fifty nights I slept through the watches without being called.

Dr. Welcker came by the next morning. He was pleased at my appearance, afraid that Joshua's restlessness would keep me awake.

"The restlessness is good, you understand. It is a sign of the consciousness struggling to return. We must encourage it."

He gave me instructions and medicines and was about to leave when someone knocked at the door. I opened to a short, neatly dressed stranger.

"Mrs. Patten? I am the hotel manager, James P. Gallagher, at your service, madam." He bowed. "I regret to disturb you but there are a number of gentlemen below who are anxious to make your acquaintance. If you could just spare a moment?"

"Gentlemen? Who could they be?"

"Reporters from the newspapers, madam. Persistent fellows. They've been hanging about the lobby for some time. Perhaps it would be best to speak with them at once and have it done."

"Very well." My shoulders lifted and fell. "I can't think what they want with me."

The doctor offered to stay with the patient while I followed the manager down the stairway. I was instantly besieged by a handful of eager young men with pencils and note pads.

"Mrs. Patten, ma'am, can you tell us about Captain Patten's condition? Is it true he has brain fever?"

"I'm afraid so. The doctor is with him now."

"We hear you took over the *Neptune* and sailed her single-handedly from Cape Horn to the Golden Gate."

"It's the *Neptune's Car*, gentlemen. And her captain is Joshua Adams Patten. I did what was necessary to assist my husband when he became ill. I could not have done anything without the support of an excellent crew, and of course, Mr. Hare, the first officer."

"What's the story on Keeler, Mrs. Patten? Didn't he start out as chief mate?"

"Yes. Mr. Keeler proved untrustworthy. My husband was forced to remove him from duty."

"The way we heard it he attempted to sabotage the ship, then tried to incite the crew to mutiny. Can you tell us where he is now?"

"I'm afraid I can't. I assume he's been turned over to the authorities."

"He ain't, ma'am." One of the men spoke up. "He's disappeared. Nobody seems to know what's happened to Mr. Keeler."

How like the man, I thought, *to find a way to escape justice! Well, it doesn't greatly matter as long as he is out of our lives.*

"Mrs. Patten, you seem remarkably young to have undertaken the responsibility you did. Would it be indelicate to ask your age?"

I smiled. "It is always indelicate to ask a lady her age, sir. But since the indiscretion is committed—I am nineteen. Now, if you will excuse me—"

"Allow us to express our greatest admiration for your courage, Mrs. Patten. It is our sincere wish that the captain will quickly be restored to his lovely helpmate."

I coughed, nodded, and retreated hurriedly up the steps. "Courage," indeed! "Lovely helpmate," indeed! I smiled to myself, thinking how much I would enjoy telling Joshua about it. I was still smiling when I reentered our rooms.

chapter
23

I was now convinced that Joshua was receiving the best possible medical care. Dr. Welcker called at least twice a day and, after two weeks, overruled my objections and installed someone to watch over Joshua for a part of each day.

"You have been cooped up in these rooms since you arrived, dear lady. I will not have you falling ill as well!"

Improvement, nevertheless, was slow. I was cautioned that it might take weeks or even months before we could be certain of recovery.

Meanwhile, another worry invaded: money. True, I had been given Joshua's percentage of the cargo profits, but living in a hotel was expensive. Then there were doctor and apothecary fees and other small necessities. I would have to do something soon about my clothes—they were all too tight and I had let the seams out as far as they would go.

We could move back to the ship, of course, but for how long? Once the owners got word of Joshua's condition they would most likely appoint another captain—at least, temporarily—to take his place. The thought hurt, but it had to be faced. It would not do to keep moving Joshua. Besides, the doctor had said the continuous dampness of the waterfront might be dangerous.

The only other choice was to find more permanent but less expensive lodging in a boardinghouse. After Christmas, I decided, that's what I would do.

As the holidays approached I tried hard not to become discouraged. Manolo called to tell me he had signed onto a Chilean coal freighter so he could go home to Santiago for a visit. 'My Margueretta, she misses me," he shrugged. "So I go to keep her and *los niños* happy."

"That's very good of you, Manolo," I laughed. "Will you wish them all a wonderful Christmas for me?"

"Sí, señora! And I will tell Margueretta to say prayers for you and the señor captain every day. I know you like prayers."

"I do. Thank you."

"Maybe sometime you ask me to be steward again, sí? *Adios*, señora. *Hasta la vista*."

"*Hasta la vista*," I echoed. . . . Until we meet again.

Dr. Welcker asked me to share Christmas dinner with his family, but I said I was unwilling to leave Joshua and he seemed to understand. When the day came, I dressed as festively as my limited wardrobe would allow, brushed my hair into a shining crown, and, as a final touch, fastened on the jade necklace Joshua had given me. Then I sat by the bed to read the story of the nativity and talk, softly, of days gone by.

"Remember last Christmas, Joshua, aboard the *Neptune's Car?* How miserable I was! I blamed it all on Louise Jordan-Chadwick, but she was only part of the problem. It was the shock, I think, of suddenly realizing how empty Christmas is when the trimmings are taken away—all those safe, comfortable things I'd always surrounded myself with.

"And now look at me—expecting a baby! And you lying there ill. Stranded without family or friends. Hardly any money or clothes. Not even sure what's going to happen next. No trimmings. But for the first time in my life, Joshua, I am really, genuinely celebrating Christmas."

Smiling, I lifted Joshua's hand and held it against my cheek. "Next year, my love, we will celebrate the birth of our Lord together, you and our baby and I. And no one in the whole world will know more joy."

When the doctor asked me my plans for the future, during that week following Christmas, I was startled.

"I was going to bring the subject up myself. I've decided to move to a boarding house, and I need your advice. Is there anything suitable you can recommend?"

"I know of no boarding houses suitable for a lady whose confinement is approaching and who has, on top of that, a dangerously ill husband."

"But Joshua's getting better. The blindness and deafness sometimes lift for a while. Like the time I read the newspaper article to him about the *Intrepid* making port eleven days after us. I'm sure he heard me, because he smiled. And once I caught his eyes following me around the room."

The doctor shook his head, but I went on. "The baby isn't due for three months. That's why it's important to get settled in another place now, while I can still—"

"Dear Mrs. Patten, I must be blunt. It has now been six weeks since your ship arrived, with far less improvement in your husband's condition than I hoped for. We cannot be sure that he will be alive in another three months."

"*No!*" I cried, shocked. "Don't say that! He will be alive, I know it!"

"All right." He held up his hands. "Think about yourself, then. This is your first child. Do you not wish for the support of a familiar place, loving friends and family, at such a time?"

"Of course I do, but—"

"I have a suggestion. Why do you not go home? Back to Boston?"

A terrible longing swept over me. "If only we could!"

"I am quite certain that steamship travel would not affect the captain's condition. There are many excellent physicians in the East who might help him, perhaps provide new treatments."

"You don't understand, doctor. It's the money. We haven't even enough to stay here, never mind pay for steamship fares." I shook my head. "I'm sorry. I didn't mean to tell you that."

"It is right that you should." He rose heavily and placed a hand on my shoulder. "We are friends, are we not? Perhaps you are not quite so alone as you imagine."

I had no idea what he meant. A few days later when the doctor called he was rubbing his hands. His eyes gleamed brightly behind his spectacles.

"Good news, my dear friend! Everything is all arranged!"

"You have found another accommodation for us?"

"I have indeed, but not in this city. By this time next week you and Captain Patten shall be on your way to New York."

I gaped at him. "We can't. I told you—"

"You have, let us say, admirers who are desirous to assist you." He shrugged expansively. "Do not forget this is the city with a heart of gold."

"I would like to repay them someday, whoever they are. If I can."

But there was to be no talk of repayment, the doctor insisted. I must think only with hope of what lay ahead, and not look back.

"I have discovered that by the greatest good fortune, a friend of mine, Dr. Harris, is to be a passenger on the same ship. You may rest assured the captain will be well cared for."

I was overwhelmed by such unexpected provision. Our departure was only a few days away, so it was necessary to begin at once to settle accounts and purchase necessary items for the voyage. The difficult time came to collect the remainder of our belongings from the *Neptune's Car* and say goodbye to Mr. Hare.

The packing took longer than I expected. There were so many things—books, clothes, linen, the set of wedding china, curios from our travels. All had memories bound up in them. When I was finished I lingered in the cabin, touching each piece of furniture, struggling with my tears. Then I walked slowly through the ship for the last time.

On the quarterdeck Mr. Hare helped me down the ladder to the boat and unshipped the oars. I kept my eyes on the clipper as we pulled away.

"You'll be back, ma'am," he said gruffly. "You and the cap'n."

"Will we, Mr. Hare?"

"You're a part of the *Neptune's Car* now. Time she shows herself in New York port again you'll be out of drydock and ready to set sail."

On the wharf I turned and extended my hand. After a moment's shy hesitation he took it.

"Thank you, Mr. Hare," I said. "You have been a good friend. Thank you for everything."

The voyage East was swift and without complications. The steamship *Golden Gate* took us down the coast as far as Panama. From there we transferred to the *George Law*, crossed to the Atlantic, and continued up the eastern seaboard. On February 14, 1857, our vessel steamed into New York Harbor.

The weather was bitterly cold, with a threat of snow in the air. My mind went back with sadness to the bright July morning that we had left the harbor. Joshua had been so happy, so confident. Now, nearly eight months later, he was returning, lying helpless on a litter.

Dear God! If only we could go back to last summer, I thought. And then I felt the new life conceived within me stir, and I remembered the bond forged between myself and my Creator. And I knew that, even if it were possible, I could not wish those months to be erased.

From the Battery Hotel I sent a wire to my mother and father. I told them Joshua and I had arrived and would be traveling to Boston as soon as it could be arranged. To my great joy, my brother George came by the next train.

"George! Dearest George!" I cried as he enfolded me. "How is Elsa? And Mama and Papa and Victoria? How did you manage to get away from the shop?"

"I'm in charge now," he reminded me, "and we're all fine except for worrying about you. Elsa and I decided you'd coped on your own long enough. You're quite a heroine, you know. The newspapers are calling you the Florence Nightingale of the Ocean!"

"*Balderdash.* Since when is doing what you have to do heroic?"

He grinned. Then he became serious. "The papers warned us about Joshua's condition, but they didn't tell about yours. We had no idea. . . . I think, little sister, it's time we got you home."

When the carriage stopped in front of the little brick house on Salutation Street and Mama and Papa opened the door I didn't know whether to laugh or cry.

"Welcome home, Mary. Thank God you're here, at last!"

My mother's arms came around me, and for a moment the tiredness, the pain of the past months slipped away and I was a child again.

"I am afraid we are going to be a burden, Mama. We are practically penniless."

"You are not to worry about money or anything else until the baby comes," she responded.

But I did worry. The recent years of my father's ill health had been hard financially on the household. The addition of two adults and a newborn child would be an impossible strain. But then, out of the blue, came a miracle: the insurers of the *Neptune's Car* sent a letter expressing their gratitude for my handling of the recent voyage. Enclosed was a check for one thousand dollars.

"*You're rich!*" Victoria gasped, frankly envious. My sister had come every day to see me since my arrival, bringing her four children, and though it was a delight to see her, the visits were wearing.

Father, who sat looking over his newspaper, replied, "Hardly that, Victoria. It's the least they could do. Mary saved the underwriters ten times that amount when she kept the ship from going into Valparaiso."

"Still, they weren't obliged to give me anything," I insisted. "It's God taking care of us, Papa. We can have the best doctors for Joshua now."

Whether it was the excellent medical care he received or the change of environment, Joshua did seem to improve during that next fortnight before the baby's birth. Although his sight was still very dim, his hearing returned and he began to respond to those around him. I was convinced that he was on his way to a complete recovery.

chapter
24

Joshua Adams Patten the second took his first breath of the salt air of Boston harbor early in the morning of March the tenth.

It was a difficult delivery. Why is it that the most treasured things in life are created through pain? When my mother and sister came some hours later to ask if they should take the blanket-wrapped infant by my side to Joshua, I shook my head.

"I'll take him," I whispered.

"You? You can't get up!"

"We've waited a long time for this moment, Mama. I don't think anything could stop me."

Seeing I was determined, they let me get up and walked with me to Joshua's door. There, I took the baby and went in.

"Mary?"

Joshua, lying with his face toward the window, turned his head as I approached the bed.

"Yes, Joshua, it's me. I've brought someone to see you!" I laid the baby carefully against him, turning back the blankets.

"It's your son, my love. A fine, strong, healthy boy!"

The radiance that lit Joshua's face dissolved all my weariness. I watched silently, giving thanks to God as his trembling fingers touched the delicate curve of the infant's cheek, his lips, the shell-like ears, exploring each limb with a look of wonder.

"So . . . *small,*" he murmured finally.

"But he has the lungs of a quarterdecker. Wait till you hear him! He looks like you, Joshua. I'm sure he's going to have fair hair and blue eyes."

"Jaw's . . . square. Stubborn."

"Like mine, alas. Poor mite, what could his mother give him that was good?"

"Her heart," Joshua smiled. "The heart . . . of a lion."

"Oh, Joshua! I'm not brave. Or good, or anything else without you!" My voice broke. I wiped my eyes. "As soon as you are fit we will sail together, the three of us. He won't ever be afraid of the sea that way."

"Mary. Don't."

Don't what?" I captured the miniature fist flailing in the air.

"*Pretend.*"

I stopped playing with the baby and stared at Joshua. "I'm not pretending. You are going to get well. God promised me."

"God?"

"On the ship one night. I told God I'd never ask for anything again if you could live to see your son. He gave me a peace about it, Joshua!"

"He . . . answered your prayer. How good . . . he is!"

"But you're not well yet!" I got up from the bed. "He wouldn't bring you this far and not heal you. He can't. And you are getting better, anyone can see that."

The baby began to cry and Joshua closed his eyes, looking very tired. I picked up the child and went to the door.

"I'm not going to let you go, my love. I've fought too hard and too long. I won't let God take you from me now."

A few weeks later I came down with a fever. It was thought at first not to be serious, but as I grew worse the doctor was summoned. He diagnosed typhoid.

For four weeks I was not permitted to see my son or husband. A nurse had to be hired, and I lay fretting at my inability to help even myself.

"Look, Mary." Victoria sat by my bed, seeking to distract me by reading my mail aloud. "Here's another invitation from a women's rights group in Connecticut. They want you to go on a lecture tour!"

"Absurd," I muttered. "Why should anyone want to listen to me?"

"You're the 'Heroine of Cape Horn'! You've proved that a woman is capable of doing a man's job."

"I didn't *want* to do it."

"That's beside the point. What's the matter with you? You used to be so keen about women's rights. Besides, think of the money you could make."

I sighed. "All I want to do is get well so I can take care of my family. And then all I want is a normal life like everyone else. . . . How *is* Joshua, Victoria? Nobody tells me."

She shrugged, avoiding my eyes. "There's little to tell. He asks for you."

"Then he's still conscious?"

"Sometimes."

Fear struck my heart. I knew she was hiding something. But it was not until I walked into his room at the end of April that I found out what it was.

Joshua was tied. His wrists and ankles had been bound securely to the bedposts so that he could move no more than a few inches. When I cried out he turned his head toward me, but his eyes were wild and unseeing. There wasn't a glimmer of recognition.

My mother and father rushed in and found me still standing there in shock.

"Mary! I'm so sorry, my dear. We didn't want you to find out like this."

"Why—why is he tied?"

"It became necessary. The disease has attacked his mind. He is violent sometimes."

My father said heavily, "The doctor thinks—and so do I— that Joshua should be put into a hospital."

"*No.*"

"For his own good, lass. He has already tried to do himself an injury. He could hurt you without meaning to."

"You want to put him into a lunatic asylum! Joshua doesn't belong there. He's sick. He needs me to take care of him."

"You aren't able to take care of him any more. And neither are we."

I wept, heartbroken. "If Joshua goes into one of those places he'll never come out again!"

On his next visit the doctor told us he had located an institution where Joshua would be well cared for. I pleaded and argued, but in the end it did no good. On a beautiful spring day Joshua was taken away to the McLean Asylum in Somerville.

When I became well enough, I took a carriage out every day to see him. He did not often know who I was. Once, however, he looked directly at me and spoke. His voice was hoarse, but the words came clearly and rapidly as though he knew the precious moment of lucidity could not last.

"*Let me go, Mary,*" he said. "*With the tide. Promise me. Don't hold me back!*"

I looked at him—wasted, pale, tortured in mind and body. Every particle of my being rebelled against yielding to what I had always considered the enemy, death. Now I knew I had been wrong. The fragile wings of his spirit were beating against the cocoon of mortality. And I must set him free.

I leaned close, kissed him, and whispered, "I promise, my darling. Go, and be happy! Remember that I will love you forever."

Joshua left me very quietly on Sunday morning, July 26, 1857.

As the news spread through Boston, the vessels in the harbor lowered their colors to half mast, and the bells of all the churches tolled in the morning.

The funeral was held at Old North Church. I don't remember much of what was said. I sat in the front row with my eyes fixed blindly on the altar, seeing the young bride and groom who had knelt there together four years before. . . . *Four years?* It seemed a lifetime. I had been a child of sixteen when I uttered the words "till death do us part." That child was now a woman with a son of her own—and death, so remote on that lovely April morning, was now a reality.

After the service a procession of carriages made its way to the cemetery in Everett. I stood beside the grave with Joshua Adams in my arms.

What am I to do now, Lord? I cried in silent agony. *You've taken Joshua. Tell me how I am to go on alone!*

The minister's voice penetrated my grief. He was reading something I recognized, a psalm that had been handwritten in the back of Joshua's Bible. It was the sailor's version of Psalm 23. As I listened an inexplicable peace stole through my spirit. It came to me, with a dawning wonder, that God was giving me his answer.

The Lord is my Pilot; I shall not drift.
He lights me across the dark waters.
He steers me through the deep channels.

He keeps my log. He guides me by the
Star of holiness for his name's sake.

As I sail through the storms and tempests
of life, I will dread no danger: for you are
near me; your love and care shelter me.

You prepare a haven before me in the
homeland of eternity; you quiet the waves
with oil; my ship rides calmly.

Surely sunlight and starlight shall be
with me wherever I sail, and at the end of
my voyaging, I shall rest in the port of my God.

part 4
VOYAGE HOME

Twilight and evening bell,
　　And after that the dark!
And may there be no sadness of farewell,
　　When I embark;

For tho' from out our bourne of Time and Place
　　The flood may bear me far,
I hope to see my Pilot face to face
　　When I have crost the bar.

　　　　　—Alfred, Lord Tennyson

chapter
25

Not quite four years have gone by since Joshua's death. In some ways it seems much longer than that; in others, it is like yesterday.

The ladies of Boston somehow discovered that Joshua's illness left us in straightened circumstances. They got up a fund and presented me with a gift of fourteen hundred dollars, which I was both embarrassed and relieved to accept. Our way of life since then has been modest, but adequate. When Papa's heart failed him a year ago, Mama and I and little Joshua Adams gave up our home in Salutation Street and went to live with my brother George's family.

The splendid era of the clipper ship draws to an end. More and more we see steam-driven vessels ply the waters of Boston Bay, and I have a sad apprehension that one day soon the clouds of canvas shall disappear altogether.

There are other clouds forming on our country's horizon, black clouds of war. Mr. Lincoln, our new President, is trying hard to steer a course of peace, but the Southern states have voted to withdraw from the union. They say Mr. Lincoln is a godly man, and I pray that it is so. He shall need all of God's divine wisdom to navigate the troubled waters ahead.

As for myself, I look forward to a voyage of my own. The years since Joshua's death have been a sort of preparation for it, and though at the time I would have chosen to go with him, I cannot regret these years that I have had with my little son. I have loved him and taught him all the important things Joshua would wish him to know. But my usefulness to him nears an end. He needs to laugh and play in the clean air of the country. He must learn how to swim and fish and handle a boat as Joshua did. And he will do all those things best in Maine. I have made arrangements for his grandparents to come for him soon. It will be very hard to say goodbye, but I have tried to explain it the best way I can to his almost four-year-old mind. I believe in some measure he understands.

"You are going away for a long, long time, Mama?"

"Yes, little one," I stroked the soft blond curls, so much like his father's. "I am going on a voyage, like your Papa. Do you remember I told you how he got very sick and had to sail away, so that he could get well again?"

"You are sick, too, Mama. Are you going to the same place Papa went?"

I nodded.

"And when you get there you won't hurt any more?"

"No, I shall be very happy. And I shall tell your Papa all about the good, strong son you are!"

"Why can't I go, too?"

"I hope you will one day, my darling. But first you must grow up straight and tall. And you must learn how to steer a ship like your Papa."

"I think I will grow up fast, Mama." A sudden anxiety struck him. You won't go away till after my birthday, will you?"

I smiled reassuringly into the pale blue eyes, and held him close.

"I'll ask the Captain, shall I, and see what he says. . . ."

Are there seas in heaven, Joshua? And is there such a vessel as our *Neptune's Car?* If there is, wait for me, and we shall explore the vast and boundless reaches of eternity together!

Only one short passage yet remains. I am not afraid. I wait, impatient, for the fullness of the tide and my Captain's command. Just a little more pain and darkness, and then the Horn shall be rounded.

And I shall come at last into the shelter of your arms.

AUTHOR'S NOTE

Mary Ann Brown Patten died from consumption—tuberculosis—on March 17, 1861, only one week following her son's fourth birthday. She was not quite twenty-four. Her headstone and that of Joshua's can be found today on the grounds of Woodlawn Cemetery in Everett, Massachusetts. Perhaps a more fitting memorial, however, is the U.S. Merchant Marine Academy's Patten Hospital at Kings Point, New York, named in her honor.

The Civil War proved a disaster to the American clipper era. Dozens of the finest vessels were captured and destroyed by Confederate raiders, many others were sold abroad. In February of 1863 the *Neptune's Car* was auctioned in Liverpool. She sailed thereafter under the British flag.

CHRISTIAN HERALD ASSOCIATION AND ITS MINISTRIES

CHRISTIAN HERALD ASSOCIATION, founded in 1878, publishes The Christian Herald Magazine, one of the leading interdenominational religious monthlies in America. Through its wide circulation, it brings inspiring articles and the latest news of religious developments to many families. From the magazine's pages came the initiative for CHRISTIAN HERALD CHILDREN and THE BOWERY MISSION, two individually supported not-for-profit corporations.

CHRISTIAN HERALD CHILDREN, established in 1894, is the name for a unique and dynamic ministry to disadvantaged children, offering hope and opportunities which would not otherwise be available for reasons of poverty and neglect. The goal is to develop each child's potential and to demonstrate Christian compassion and understanding to children in need.

Mont Lawn is a permanent camp located in Bushkill, Pennsylvania. It is the focal point of a ministry which provides a healthful "vacation with a purpose" to children who without it would be confined to the streets of the city. Up to 1000 children between the age of 7 and 11 come to Mont Lawn each year.

Christian Herald Children maintains year-round contact with children by means of a *City Youth Ministry.* Central to its philosophy is the belief that only through sustained relationships and demonstrated concern can individual lives be truly enriched. Special emphasis is on individual guidance, spiritual and family counseling and tutoring. This follow-up ministry to inner-city children culminates for many in financial assistance toward higher education and career counseling.

THE BOWERY MISSION, located at 227 Bowery, New York City, has since 1879 been reaching out to the lost men on the Bowery, offering them what could be their last chance to rebuild their lives. Every man is fed, clothed and ministered to. Countless numbers have entered the 90-day residential rehabilitation program at the Bowery Mission. A concentrated ministry of counseling, medical care, nutrition therapy, Bible study and Gospel services awakens a man to spiritual renewal within himself.

These ministries are supported solely by the voluntary contributions of individuals and by legacies and bequests. Contributions are tax deductible. Checks should be made out either to CHRISTIAN HERALD CHILDREN or to THE BOWERY MISSION.

Administrative Office: 40 Overlook Drive, Chappaqua, New York 10514
Telephone: (914) 769-9000